Murder Sees All

A Myrtle Clover Mystery, Volume 27

Elizabeth Spann Craig

Published by Elizabeth Spann Craig, 2025.

MURDER SEES ALL

First edition. November 4, 2025.

ISBN: 978-1955395670

Written by Elizabeth Spann Craig.

Chapter One

Myrtle Clover stood at her front window, eyes narrowed with ferocious irritation. "This yard is completely appalling," she informed Pasha, her black feral feline companion.

Pasha narrowed her green eyes in solidarity.

"The weeds staged a coup," she said. "They sneaked over from Erma Sherman's despicable property and invaded my own patch. And Dusty has done absolutely nothing about it."

Pasha sneezed as if she were allergic to Dusty's name. Myrtle completely understood, as she was beginning to feel that way herself.

"This is all Dusty's doing. He's fallen down on the job," said Myrtle grimly.

Pasha swished her tail.

A loud rattling, squeaking sound approached Myrtle's house from the end of Magnolia Lane. "It's him!" said Myrtle. "Well, thank heaven. It certainly took him enough time. I plan on giving Dusty a piece of my mind."

But when Myrtle stepped out her front door, Pasha at her heels, Dusty's truck passed by in a cloud of black exhaust without even slowing down.

To add insult to injury, Pasha, finding some sort of delightful, delicious prey in the tall grass, bounded away.

Myrtle sighed. "There's nothing to do but call Miles. This will require a car."

The only problem was that Miles could be resistant when Myrtle tried borrowing his vehicle. It was quite annoying, since Myrtle was an excellent and quite cautious driver. Nor did Miles particularly want to chauffeur Myrtle when she had special missions like tailing Dusty's truck. She'd have to come up with a more appealing reason for borrowing the car, she supposed.

Myrtle took out her phone and called Miles. "Good morning," she sang out.

Miles instantly sounded suspicious. "Good morning. Was there something you needed?"

"Goodness, I don't have to need something whenever I phone a friend. I simply wanted to see if you'd like to go for a drive. It's a beautiful day. I could pack us a lunch."

The suspicious tone deepened in Miles's voice. "This is rather out of the blue, isn't it? Just yesterday, you were saying you wanted to work in your yard. That your yard was getting on your last nerve. In fact, you were saying you were going to hunt down Dusty and force him to mow your grass and spray your weeds."

"Did I? It certainly sounds as if I was loquacious yesterday." Myrtle tried to keep the irritation out of her voice. "At any rate, you're right. I was obsessed with my yard yesterday. That's precisely the reason I want to go for a drive. That way, I won't be standing at the window and fretting over it."

Miles seemed to be weighing Myrtle's words for veracity. "I suppose I could drive you," he said, sounding churlish.

"Excellent!" she said. "Shall I meet you outside?"

"Right now?"

The irritation she'd managed to keep at bay now crept into her voice. "Right now."

A few moments later, Myrtle and Miles were seated in Miles's car with Miles at the wheel. "Let's go," said Myrtle impatiently. "That way." She gestured toward the lake, which had appeared to be the direction her wayward yardman was heading.

Miles set out at a sedate pace, the sort of speed that Myrtle ordinarily found pleasing. Today, however, she was afraid she'd lose track of Dusty. "Maybe a bit faster."

Miles looked at her in surprise. "Faster? You never want to go faster. I've seen turtles creep faster than you drive."

"Today is different. I want to remove myself from my premises as quickly as possible."

Miles pushed the accelerator a bit more, rising to a speed that was closer to the speed limit. He turned on the radio to a public radio jazz station. While he was gently tapping the steering wheel in time to the music, Myrtle scanned the horizon for Dusty's decrepit vehicle.

Finally, she spotted it. "Stop the car!" she ordered.

Dusty's truck was no longer shambling down the road, but parked in front of none other than Victoria Ashworth's restored mansion on the opposite side of the lake from Myrtle. She was treated to the horrifying spectacle of Victoria serving Dusty lemonade in a crystal glass as she pointed out various features of her landscape.

"He's *cheating* on me," gritted Myrtle from between her teeth. "That scoundrel."

Miles glowered at her. "You were hunting down Dusty this whole time."

Myrtle had the grace to look slightly sheepish. "I wanted to get to the bottom of the issue and wasn't sure how else to approach it, Miles. I appreciate the ride."

Miles gave a stiff nod. He looked over at Dusty. "He barely even looks like Dusty. He's wearing that old uniform he's dug out once or twice when he wants to make a good impression. And it looks like he's shaved."

"Which is rare." Myrtle's gaze hadn't left the tableau in the mansion's garden. "Dusty certainly seems very attentive to Victoria."

Miles said dryly, "You sound as if you might be jealous."

"I'm green with envy! I want Dusty to be attentive to *my* yard. My yard, which looks as if could serve as the setting for a Tarzan movie. Instead, he's clean-shaven, gawking at Victoria Ashworth's rose garden, and wearing a uniform. It's outrageous."

Then, to Myrtle's horror, Victoria left the yardman to head inside her tremendous home as Dusty started working on the grounds with uncharacteristic vigor and enthusiasm.

"The very idea!" huffed Myrtle.

"We've seen that hard-working side of Dusty before."

"But never in my yard," said Myrtle. "It's all very annoying."

Just then something, perhaps the glint of sunlight off the metal of Miles's car, caught Dusty's attention. They could see him frown at the stopped vehicle and put his hand up to shield his eyes to take a look. Myrtle and Miles ducked below the dashboard with surprising agility, considering their age. When they dared look up again, Dusty was turned away from them, ginger-ly trimming a rose bush.

"I really don't know why we're hiding," said Miles. "It's not like you. You're a very straight-forward person. I'd have thought you'd have stomped over there, accosted Dusty, and demanded to know why he's neglecting your yard in favor of Victoria's."

Myrtle said in a sour voice, "Because Dusty should realize on his own that this is garden-variety betrayal."

"No pun intended."

"Puns are always intended," said Myrtle with a sniff. "Let's leave."

On the way back, Myrtle was muttering darkly to herself. "I'd hoped it was just his usual laziness. Instead, his head's been turned by Victoria."

"You think he has a crush on Victoria?" asked Miles.

"No, no, of course not. I think Dusty has a crush on Victoria's *yard*. I've suspected that part of Dusty's problem, not all of it, mind you, is the tedium of caring for the same uninspired yards day in and day out. But Victoria's yard is something new and different."

Miles said, "I don't know if I'd even refer to Victoria's space as a yard at all."

"What would you call it?"

"Oh, something like a 'garden' or 'grounds.' Definitely some-thing grander than a yard," said Miles in a thoughtful voice. He glanced swiftly across at Myrtle. "I'm a bit surprised at how cross you are over Dusty's elopement. He drives you so crazy that I'd have thought you wouldn't really mind having to find a new yardman."

"If you dig around in your memory a little, you'll remember the reason. It involves money and availability."

Miles said, "Ah. That's right. Dusty is cheap. And he's one of the few yardmen who has open spots on his schedule."

"Make that the *only* yardman with open spots. Even Tiny is booked solid." Myrtle's face was brooding as she gazed unseeingly out the window as Miles pulled the car into her driveway. "And now Victoria has stolen him away with lemonade, fancy glassware, and a big yard."

Miles said, "Why don't you just talk it out with Dusty? Maybe you'll find that he's just stepping in for her usual guy."

"Which doesn't explain the horrid state of my yard over the past several weeks. No, I believe he's decided to be Victoria's permanent yardman."

Miles said, "Although perhaps 'gardener' would be a better term. Considering the property we're speaking of." He paused. "Why would *Victoria* choose Dusty, of all people?"

"Because he'll be excellent with caring for her yard. But also, because she likely faced the same conundrum. No one else was available."

"Couldn't she have simply bribed someone away?" asked Miles. "I'd imagine Tiny would be imminently bribable."

"Clearly, the others were more loyal to their clients than their wallets," said Myrtle, sounding peeved. "Again, it's all very aggravating."

Since Myrtle seemed to make no move to open her door, Miles said helpfully, "We're at your house."

"So we are." Myrtle sighed. "Would you like to trek through the jungle and come inside? We could watch our tape of *Tomor-*

row's Promise and have something to eat. I feel like having something salty."

Minutes later, Myrtle and Miles sat down in Myrtle's living room. Myrtle had made them a simple snack of saltine crackers and white cheese. Miles had learned simple was better when it came to Myrtle and food preparation.

While his friend was still fumbling with the television remote, he asked, "I think you might actually miss Dusty."

"Certainly not," said Myrtle coldly. "I miss having a yard that doesn't make my house look abandoned."

"But it's more than that. I think you and Dusty get along better than you put on."

Myrtle gave Miles an exasperated look. "I get along better with Dusty than I do with Puddin. That's about as far as it goes."

Puddin was married to Dusty and served as Myrtle's housekeeper. She was deplorable at her job and lazy on top of it.

"Well, that's a given. Puddin is difficult. But Dusty does a good job," said Miles.

"Dusty does a good job when he actually makes it over here. I feel as if I have to threaten or bribe those two to get any actual work done. It's completely exhausting." Myrtle jabbed at the remote with her finger, clearly done with the subject. "Now, let's watch our show."

They were a few minutes into the soap opera when Miles frowned. "This storyline is quite confusing."

"The one with Marcus in it?"

Miles nodded. "Can you remind me how it all works? I suspect I must have gotten up to get more tea when the last show was on."

Myrtle hit the pause button. "Remember the rich Blackwood family patriarch? Luciano?"

"The one who looks like the wizard of Oz?"

Myrtle said, "Not that one. The one who looks like the British version of Santa Claus. Father Christmas."

"Oh, that's right. Yes. So Luciano died, I believe. In a boating accident."

Myrtle said, "Yes. But Marcus is his identical twin brother."

"I think this soap opera has far too many twins in it. It pushes the boundary for what's believable."

"The whole thing pushes believability, Miles. It's intended to be an escape. Anyway, Marcus has been impersonating Luciano to steal the inheritance. But Luciano isn't dead at all. He's being held captive by his wife in his own wine cellar. She's been slowly poisoning him with arsenic in his daily vitamins."

Miles sighed.

Myrtle continued. "The twist is that his wife believes the man she's holding captive is her brother-in-law Marcus, *not* her husband, Luciano. She doesn't believe his protestations."

"This is absurd."

"But riveting. Just watch."

They watched the next scene, and Miles had to agree that it was quite riveting, despite the absurdity. There was something about Luciano insisting that he was Luciano that was all very dramatic.

The action was just reaching a crescendo when the doorbell rang. Myrtle and Miles both jumped in their seats. Myrtle said, "You'd think we were about to be thrown into the wine cellar with Luciano. It's just a doorbell."

It was Wanda at the door. Wanda was Myrtle's dear friend, a cousin to Miles, and a gifted psychic. She gave them a gap-toothed grin. "Watchin' yer show?"

"We are, but we'd rather be visiting with you," said Myrtle, eagerly motioning Wanda inside and to a chair. "Let's get you something to eat. Miles and I were just enjoying a snack of saltine crackers and cheese."

Wanda shook her head. "I'm okay, thanks."

This startled Myrtle. She was accustomed to Wanda coming in her house and inhaling any food she put in front of her. "Aren't you feeling all right?"

"Jest fine. Gotta run over to see somebody. Wanted to tell you about it first."

Myrtle's brow crinkled. She sat down in her armchair again. "Gracious. That sounds ominous."

Wanda looked serious, herself. "It's jest that it's over at that mansion."

Myrtle sat up straighter. "Victoria's mansion?"

"There aren't too many others," Miles pointed out helpfully.

Wanda gave a bob of her head. "It's that one. Knew you was upset about Dusty bein' there."

Myrtle and Miles no longer even blinked when Wanda offered up these startling examples of her abilities. Myrtle said, "You mean the fact that Dusty is a complete and utter traitor for abandoning me and my pitiful yard? Don't worry, Wanda. If you're going there, it's a totally different scenario. You don't work for me. You're not leaving me in a bad situation. And, I presume, this probably has something to do with a gig."

Wanda looked relieved. "That's right. Wants me to do a party." She shifted uncomfortably in her seat. "Don't wanna do it. But I could use the money. Dan asked fer some money."

Now Myrtle's expression darkened. Crazy Dan was Wanda's nutty brother. He was fond of spending money, but Myrtle thought Wanda was rid of him when he'd suddenly married.

Miles looked concerned, too. "Surely you don't have to support Dan and his wife? You've been supporting him far too long."

Wanda sighed. "Yep. But it's jest fer a bit. He got hisself into a credit card problem. Asked me to bail him out."

Myrtle said, "Well, I certainly hope this isn't going to continue being a thing. That man doesn't deserve a cent from you."

"He's done tore up the credit card. Says this is it."

Myrtle nodded. "Excellent. So money is required."

"Ain't it always the way?"

Miles cleared his throat, looking uncomfortable as usual when conversation drifted to finances. "Wanda, I hope you know I could spot you some money. Make a donation, so to speak."

Myrtle said, "I would too, Wanda. Except retirement for teachers isn't the same as for urban planners."

"Civil engineers," said Miles between gritted teeth.

Wanda gave him a sad smile. "Know yew would. Cain't take it. Need to do this on my own. But thank yew."

Myrtle said, "Going back to Victoria, who's now my archenemy because of her theft of Dusty. What precisely is she having you do, Wanda? I hate that it's making you uncomfortable. You don't enjoy working in groups, as I recall."

Wanda sighed. "It's a party. She'll have folks over. Wanted me to dew a séance. Don't much like 'em. Told her I'd do for-toons instead."

"No, I wouldn't suppose you would like séances. I know you find this sort of work taxing." Myrtle knit her brows. "That Victoria!" Then she said, "Why don't Miles and I come along? For support."

Miles shot her a look that clearly articulated that attending a séance at Victoria's mansion was the last thing in the world he wanted to do. Myrtle ignored it.

"Yew would?" asked Wanda, looking relieved. Then she hesitated. "Yew wouldn't be invited."

"Miles and I would crash the party."

Now Miles was positively alarmed. "No. Absolutely no party crashing."

"It's probably going to be such a large crowd that she wouldn't even notice," said Myrtle.

Miles gave her a withering look. "I think Victoria would notice when we sat down at a table."

"We'd probably blend in."

"We'd be the oldest ones there," Miles pointed out.

Wanda didn't want them to squabble. "Don't think it'll work out, but thank yew."

Myrtle, however, was determined. When Myrtle had a bee in her bonnet, she was like a bloodhound with a scent. "It *will* work out. This is what we'll do. Miles and I will loiter outside the home, on the premises. That way we'll be safely in the background. We won't serve as a distraction, but you'll know we're there supplying you moral support."

Miles looked only marginally more pleased at the idea of trespassing on Victoria's property instead of party crashing.

Wanda, however, was quite happy again. "Good idea. That'll work. Sendin' me gud vibes."

Myrtle said, "How exactly did this job come up?"

Wanda sighed. "Reckon through the newspaper."

This made a good deal of sense. Wanda wrote the horoscopes for the *Bradley Bugle*. Or, more accurately, Wanda dictated the horoscopes to Myrtle. Wanda's horoscopes weren't the usual fare. They were specific and insightful. The editor of the paper, Sloan Jones, was certain the feature was solely responsible for the paper's healthy number of subscribers.

"Speaking of the newspaper," Miles said thoughtfully, "didn't I read something some time ago about Victoria's home?"

Myrtle said, "You certainly did. She's having it converted into a bed-and-breakfast. But it's not going to be a cozy sort of place. She wants it to be upscale and ritzy." Myrtle spat out the words as if *upscale* and *ritzy* were akin to contagious diseases that might spread throughout Bradley if left unchecked.

There was a loud crowing sound outside that startled Miles and even made Wanda raise her eyebrows. Myrtle rolled her eyes. "Wanda, you seem to know what that is."

Wanda nodded. "'Fraid so."

"It sounded like a rooster," said Miles. "Surely, it wasn't a rooster."

Myrtle said, "We should take a look outside."

Myrtle, Miles, and Wanda stepped out onto Myrtle's small front porch. There they were treated with the unexpected sight of Myrtle's daughter-in-law, Elaine, pursuing a rooster in Myrtle's front yard with a small blur that was Myrtle's grandson, Jack, racing behind her and laughing uproariously.

Miles hurried over to corral the small animal, who didn't appear grateful in the slightest. It struggled in his arms, pecking ferociously at him.

"Sorry, sorry!" said Elaine, gasping from laughter and from running. "Scotty, what were you thinking? Bad boy!"

Scotty didn't seem repentant in the slightest. Elaine carefully collected him from Miles, who looked vastly relieved by the transfer. Wanda hid a grin.

"How's life on the farm?" asked Myrtle.

Elaine pushed a strand of hair out of her face. "For the most part, it's all going very well. Except Scotty isn't fond of his accommodations. Or his feed. Or the other chickens."

"Doesn't like Red neither, I reckon," said Wanda knowingly.

"That's the truth," said Elaine. "In fact, I think Scotty despises him."

A smile curved around Myrtle's lips at the mention of her son. Red was often a thorn in her side. He was fond of threatening her with incarceration in Greener Pastures Retirement Home, an abhorrent abomination. Consequently, she'd retaliate by having Dusty pull out her collection of garden gnomes, which Red considered an equal abomination. The thought of Dusty made her scowl again. She focused back on Red. "So the rooster isn't crazy about the man of the house?"

"He's not. Scotty seems to think their roles should be reversed and that Red should be in the chicken coop at night, and he should be in the house."

Myrtle said, "I'm sure Red doesn't care much for the rooster's opinion."

"No," said Elaine with a laugh. "He doesn't seem to."

Jack gave Myrtle a hug on one leg, grinning up at her. His nose looked a bit runny and his hair was askew, but he couldn't have looked more perfect to Myrtle. "The most important question," said Myrtle, "is how Scotty does with my darling grandson."

Elaine smiled. "He loves Jack and vice-versa. Actually, Scotty terrorizes everyone except Jack. He's the one exception."

To prove this, the rooster started pecking at Elaine and squawking at her indignantly.

"I better go," she said in a hurry. "He needs to get back in the yard. And I need to continue researching calming treats for chickens. I'm certain there must be some sort of herbal remedy I can try." She gave them all a quick goodbye before ducking out with Jack in tow.

"Reckon I should leave too," drawled Wanda. "Gotta start getting' ready for that party."

Myrtle said, "Just remember we have a plan. Miles and I will lurk in the background, sending good vibes."

Miles looked as if his head might be hurting. "No loitering."

"Well of *course* we'll be loitering. We just won't be *trespassing*. There's no way for the plan to move forward without loitering being involved," said Myrtle.

"Thank yew both fer this," said Wanda.

After she left, Miles looked warily at Myrtle. "You seem wound up about something."

"Me? Heavens no. Why on earth would I be wound up about anything?"

Miles said, "Knowing you, I'm guessing it has something to do with an errant invitation from Victoria. You're upset at being overlooked."

"It's difficult to overlook me," said Myrtle. "I'm about six feet tall."

"I just know that you've gotten your nose out of joint when you haven't gotten invited to events in the past."

"A rarity," said Myrtle with a sniff. There was a Christmas cookie exchange that did come to mind.

"It's probably not that big of a gathering," said Miles. "Nor something you'd want to attend."

Myrtle did want to attend, as a matter of fact. She very much wanted to. For one thing, she wanted to see the inside of the renovated house. The last time she'd gone in there was when she'd been a child. Since she was an octogenarian, that had been many moons ago. She had the vague memory of a rather stuffy place with the smell of old leather-bound books and lots of dark, looming Victorian furniture. Naturally, she had her pride to consider, however. She would not admit wanting to go to the party.

"No, it's not something I'd want to attend. You're right, Miles. Victoria isn't my cup of tea at all. We're better off lurking in the bushes outside."

Miles looked alarmed again, and Myrtle quickly said, "Just kidding. Heavens, Miles, you know we won't be doing any lurking. Now, let's watch the rest of our show."

Chapter Two

It was later that same afternoon when Myrtle made her way to the mailbox, muttering darkly about Bradley's postal carrier. The man delivered mail whenever the spirit moved him. It could be before lunch, at sunset, or never. Today she'd only bothered checking because she'd heard his jeep's death rattle announcing its approach.

When she opened the mailbox, a fancy envelope fairly leaped out at her. Expensive paper and with Victoria's return address. But not a postmark or stamp in sight.

"Well, well," said Myrtle under her breath as she examined the evidence. "Someone's been playing mailman."

Inside was an engraved invitation to tomorrow night's party, complete with a handwritten note in flowing script: *Please bring a plus one! Looking forward to seeing you! Victoria.*

The excessive exclamation points alone were enough to raise Myrtle's blood pressure.

"Hmph." Someone had clearly tattled about her being overlooked. Wanda was the obvious suspect, though it seemed unlike her to volunteer information to Victoria.

Myrtle decided to share this important development with Miles immediately. Her cane beat a determined rhythm on the sidewalk as she marched to his house and jabbed the doorbell with authority.

Nothing.

She jabbed again, adding an impatient foot-tap to her repertoire.

Still nothing.

"Looking for Miles?"

Myrtle spun around, mentally cursing her lack of vigilance. Erma Sherman, her horrid neighbor, lurked behind her like a persistent rash. Once Erma attached herself to a conversation like a limpet, surgical intervention was required for removal.

"Obviously," said Myrtle curtly. "I'll call him instead."

"Maybe he fell down," suggested Erma with ghoulish enthusiasm.

Myrtle's glare could have wilted kudzu. "He's fine. Just busy, I'm sure."

"We should check on him. He could be trapped on the floor, unable to reach the phone, slowly—"

"Miles is fitter than both of us combined," Myrtle snapped, though Erma's morbid speculation was worming its way into her brain.

Just then, the door opened. Miles appeared, looking puzzled but perfectly upright.

"Myrtle?" he asked, frowning in confusion at the sight of Myrtle with her nemesis.

"Important business! Goodbye, Erma." Myrtle practically shoved Miles back inside and slammed the door with the finality of a coffin lid.

Miles blinked at his friend. "What was all that about? What important business?"

Myrtle waved the invitation at him. "We've been invited to Victoria's party."

"*We* have? Or *you* have?"

Myrtle said impatiently, "You're invited as my plus-one. Although I do despise that expression. What's wrong with putting 'and guest' on an invitation the way we all used to?"

Miles didn't appear to want to delve into semantics for the time being. "The timing seems suspect."

Myrtle sniffed. "Victoria probably realized her error and quickly rectified it. Or her invitation was simply delayed in the mail."

"Local mail?"

Myrtle said, "You've seen the lackadaisical way the carrier has been delivering lately. If we sent our post by carrier pigeon it would arrive quicker."

"Do you happen to have the invitation on you?"

Myrtle did. It had been stuffed absentmindedly into one of her generous pockets in her slacks. However, she didn't want Miles to note there was no stamp or postmark on the envelope, so she simply shook her head.

Miles sighed. "I have the feeling Victoria felt pressured to invite you. And the plus-one."

"For heaven's sake, Miles, it doesn't matter, does it? The point is that Wanda, our dear Wanda, is in need of our support.

Now we have a legitimate invitation to the event, and we must be there."

Miles looked gloomy. "Is it a suit type of party?"

"You practically wear a suit as pajamas! You're forever in a suit."

It wasn't quite true, but it wasn't far off, either. Miles's daily attire, which functioned nearly like a uniform, was comprised of carefully ironed khaki pants and a button-down shirt. His shoes and his belt matched perfectly. He looked perpetually ready for a job interview at a small-town bank. Or someone who could jump in to give an emergency PowerPoint presentation at a moment's notice. Myrtle's own comfortable attire appeared positively bohemian by comparison.

Miles sighed again. "So a suit?"

"No, I can't imagine a suit is necessary at such an event. The entire premise is local society types oohing and ahhing over poor Wanda and squealing over palm readings."

Despite hearing he wouldn't require a suit, Miles looked even more morose. "What time should I pick you up?"

"It starts at seven, so let's say 6:45." She frowned, cocking her head. "What's that noise?"

After a few moments, it was clear it was Dusty's truck, making its usual squealing and gasping as it hiccupped down the road. Then the noise stopped.

Myrtle's face lit up. "Miles! He's at my house! Dusty's going to cut my lawn."

Miles smiled at her. "He didn't want to leave you in the lurch. He's a good man, underneath it all."

Myrtle practically skipped out the door and down the side-walk to her own home, two doors down. Fortunately, there was no Erma encounter this time since she'd completely forgotten to watch out for her.

But when Myrtle arrived at her house, she found, not the wizened Dusty, but a sullen Puddin standing in her yard. The grass was so tall, you couldn't even see her knees.

"Puddin," said Myrtle in disappointment. It wasn't that she didn't want Puddin to come clean. It was more that the yard, for once, was in much poorer shape than the interior of Myrtle's house.

"Yep," said Puddin. She nodded her head resentfully at the door. "Gonna let me in?"

"Of course. I do have some dust bunnies that need attending to. But I have to say I'm surprised to see you here. Your presence usually isn't voluntary. In fact, I ordinarily have to practically extort you to make you come clean."

"Dusty made me come," snarled Puddin. She stooped to pick up various ratty-looking cleaning supplies that had been invisible in the grass, which was tall enough to hide a small child or a moderately sized garden gnome. "Feels like if I clean, you won't be mad at both of us, just him."

Myrtle opened the door and gestured her inside. She was already coming up with questions to ask Puddin about Dusty's arrangement with Victoria. If there was one thing she absolutely knew about Puddin, it's that she was willing to be distracted from accomplishing any work.

Myrtle continued. "I'm equally surprised that Dusty dropped you off without tackling the jungle in my yard."

Puddin raised her chin. "I'm mad at Dusty."

This wasn't completely unheard of. "What's he done now?"

Puddin was only too happy to rant about her husband. "Wants me to work for that Victoria."

Myrtle couldn't believe Dusty, who was cleverer than he appeared, would dream that a woman like Victoria, in a house like that, would even consider the services of someone like Puddin. "How does he plan to make that happen? Doesn't Victoria have Bitsy or a comparable housekeeper already employed?" Bitsy was Puddin's cousin and sort of the anti-Puddin. She was excellent at what she did and was reliable, to boot.

"Wants me to audition for her," said Puddin furiously. "Wants me to go over there an' clean. For nuthin'!"

The scheme suddenly became clear to Myrtle. "I see. So Dusty wants you to go to Victoria's house, put in a good deal of hard labor, and have Victoria hire you on for good." It seemed a very optimistic plan. Plus, Myrtle wasn't altogether sure Puddin could fake hard work. It didn't appear to be in her genetic make-up.

Puddin's pale face looked peeved. "Dusty don't get it. That woman ain't gonna want me over there. She can have somebody else, for what she pays."

"Which takes me back to my original question. Doesn't Victoria employ other housekeepers already?"

Puddin shrugged. "Lost Brenda Stamper 'cause Brenda done broke her back."

"Gracious," said Myrtle mildly.

Puddin shrugged again. "So no. She's got nobody."

"Dusty clearly saw an opening and decided you'd be the perfect candidate."

Puddin took a seat on Myrtle's sofa, happy to be diverted from cleaning. "Yep."

"Tell me why Victoria secured Dusty's services. That's quite a remarkable procurement, isn't it?"

Puddin scowled at her. "Wish you'd speak English."

"Why did Victoria hire Dusty? Dusty is lazy and impossible to reach."

Puddin said, "Oh, she needed somebody. Dusty was free."

"It doesn't explain how Dusty made a good enough impression to get hired."

Puddin said, "Dusty knows how to do good if he has to."

"I sense you're both saving for another trip to Myrtle Beach." Myrtle sighed. "The problem is that my yard looks horrid. I wish he'd stayed instead of dropping you off."

But Puddin didn't seem to care about Myrtle's yard issues. She was more focused on her upcoming housekeeping audition. And, apparently, not attending it.

Myrtle studied Puddin thoughtfully. "You're acting rather out of character, Puddin."

Puddin narrowed her eyes. "Nope."

"Yes, you are. Not in *every* way. Obviously, you always avoid doing any major work."

Puddin didn't disagree.

"However, in my experience, the desire to make what's likely a good deal of money would have made you at least try to adapt to doing hard work." Myrtle tilted her head to one side. "There must be something else."

"Nope," said Puddin again.

Unbeknownst to both of them, Pasha had followed them in. She now made herself known by wrapping herself around Puddin's ankles. Puddin shrieked and jumped on top of Myrtle's sofa. Pasha's green eyes gleamed with amusement.

"That witch cat! Where'd she come from?"

Myrtle said, "From outdoors, like she always does. And now I think I might know why you have such antipathy toward working for Victoria."

"English," said Puddin between gritted teeth as she gingerly dismounted the sofa, glaring at the black cat as she did so.

"I know why you don't want to work for Victoria. For heaven's sake, Puddin, I'm speaking your native tongue. The words are completely understandable in context. Anyway, as I was saying, you don't want to work for Victoria because you're afraid."

Puddin made a scoffing sound, but Myrtle had the feeling she'd hit the nail on the head. She continued. "That's it, isn't it? You don't want to be in that house."

Puddin was quiet for a few moments. Then she said, "That house ain't right. Some places got memories."

"That's very fanciful of you, Puddin. The house is just an inanimate object. It's not alive."

But Puddin's expression was mulish. She clearly didn't believe Myrtle. "Ain't goin' there."

Myrtle said, "I'm going there myself tomorrow. Victoria is having a party, and Miles and I are invited to attend. I can promise you everything will be fine."

Puddin shook her head. "Don't go. You don't wanna go there."

"I do want to go there. And I am. You'll see that nothing will happen aside from Wanda getting exhausted by having to perform on Victoria's whim."

Puddin looked startled. "Witchy Wanda's going to be there?"

"I simply can't believe the amount of nonsense and foolishness I have to put up with regularly. Wanda is not a witch. Wanda is a friend with an unusual gift. Victoria asked her to come to the party so she could give fortunes to her friends." Myrtle felt a wave of sympathy for Wanda again. Victoria was making her the party equivalent of a clown making balloon animals.

"Don't go," said Puddin firmly. "Bad stuff will happen."

"Because the house isn't right? Because it has memories? Really, Puddin."

But Puddin remained stubbornly convinced Myrtle should spend the next evening at home. She continued telling Myrtle this throughout the time she spent housekeeping and until Dusty finally whisked her away in his deathtrap of a truck.

The next evening, Myrtle critically surveyed her closet as if it had personally offended her. She wasn't at all sure what one wore to this type of party. She supposed her funeral pantsuit would be all right. Black was versatile, and if things went as poorly as Puddin expected, she'd already be dressed for the occasion. Though perhaps that was overly pessimistic. Then again, considering many of the social events she'd attended had resulted in corpses, perhaps pessimism was required.

There was a peal of thunder, and Myrtle frowned. It all seemed rather cliché to be going to a party at a house with "memories" to watch a psychic during a thunderstorm. But the thunder continued, with lightning interspersing the booms.

A wild crowing commenced outside, and Myrtle could hear Elaine's voice calling, "Scotty! Scotty!"

Myrtle abandoned her closet to help Elaine. Unfortunately, at that moment, her lights went out at the same time her doorbell rang. "Stuff and nonsense," muttered Myrtle as she grabbed her cane and maneuvered her way to the door in the dim light trickling in from the windows.

When Myrtle swung the door open, Miles gave a very un-Miles-like shriek as Scotty came rocketing at them in a tempest of offended squawks and flapping wings, as if the storm had personally insulted his dignity.

Pasha, who'd left when Puddin had, used the opportunity to hurtle back into Myrtle's house after the errant rooster.

"No, Pasha!" said Myrtle. Although she felt bad about scolding the cat, who was only doing what cats do.

Pasha gave her a reproachful look before retreating to a spot where she could keep a gleaming eye on the rooster.

Rain exploded from the sky then, driving sideways through the doorway until Elaine rushed in and wrestled the door shut. "There's Mama's good boy," she crooned at the rooster. "Come here, Scotty."

But Scotty was having none of it. He puffed up like an indignant feather duster, fixing Pasha with the sort of glare usually reserved for mortal enemies. Pasha, unimpressed by his theatrics, settled into her evening grooming routine with studied nonchalance. This casual dismissal only further enraged the rooster, who began marching back and forth across Myrtle's living room like Napoleon planning his next conquest.

Another peal of thunder sounded, this one shaking Myrtle's small house in the process. The door opened again, and Myrtle's son, Red, stood there, his graying red hair plastered to his head in the rain.

"Where's Jack?" asked Myrtle, her darling grandson always at the forefront of her mind.

Elaine said, "Oh, he has a playdate at a friend's house. Although that should be wrapping up shortly."

Red's face was just as thunderous as the storm outside. "Where's that bird?"

Elaine said, "Scotty?"

"Are there any other birds hanging out over here?" asked Red.

Scotty flew at Red, flapping his wings at his legs and pecking him.

"I think he blames you for the storm," said Elaine helpfully.

Red muttered something under his breath that thankfully couldn't be heard. He stooped to grab the rooster, but Scotty proved surprisingly elusive, dodging with the agility of a prize-fighter. Instead, he headed toward Miles, who'd strategically positioned himself in the farthest corner of the small room. He watched with alarm as Scotty approached. But the bird seemed to take to Miles, or at least appeared to find him nonthreatening. It stood by him, glaring at everyone in the room.

Miles gingerly scooped it up, handing it over to Elaine, who'd reached for it. "I'll put him back in the coop," she said quickly, bolting out into the pouring rain.

Red wiped the rain off his face, sighing. Myrtle felt a rare sympathy for him. "Elaine's new hobby seems unusually aggressive."

"That bird's going to end up being Sunday dinner if he keeps this up," said Red.

Myrtle looked at her watch. "Heavens, I need to start getting ready."

"Ready for what?" asked Red.

Miles looked uncomfortable.

Myrtle said, "Miles and I are joining Wanda at a party Victoria Ashworth is giving."

Red knit his brows. "Well now, y'all make an unlikely trio for a party at Victoria's house. Or should I say Victoria's *mansion*?"

Myrtle pressed her lips together in annoyance. Then she said, "Miles and I are perfectly presentable for an event at a fine home."

"Of course you are. But Victoria's crowd tends to be a lot younger. The sort of people who spend a lot of time taking pictures of themselves on social media."

"They're called 'selfies,'" said Myrtle, sounding caustic.

Red surveyed his mother. "You're not wearing what you currently have on, are you? I'm no fashion expert, but I don't think elastic-waisted pants and a shirt you wore while gardening are going to cut it."

"Of course they won't. I have no intention of wearing these clothes. I was in the process of finding something suitable when Scotty decided to visit." Myrtle looked down at her shirt. Red was right. She'd somehow managed to get specks of red clay on it while pulling weeds in her backyard. It was all most annoying. She wasn't even sure why she was trying to make a dent in the weeds. They'd increased exponentially along with the height of the grass. "I'd really better get going, Red. Miles is waiting on me."

Miles gave Red an apologetic look.

Red frowned. "Actually, Mama, there's something I wanted to bring up with you. Did you fire Dusty?"

"What? Of course not! You know I can't fire Dusty. He's the only yardman I can afford in this town. Well, I might afford Tiny, but you know he's always booked out."

Red said, "Is Dusty mortally ill, then?"

"Certainly not!"

"You wouldn't happened to have cooked a meal for him or anything?" pushed Red.

"What are you rambling on about?" Myrtle demanded.

Miles made some strangled sounds behind Myrtle, and she turned to eye him suspiciously.

Red rolled his eyes. "Mama, I just want to know why your yard is so completely out of control. That's all."

Myrtle raised her chin. "It's because Dusty is derelict in duty. As usual."

"Well, Dusty's lazy, but the grass has never been this tall." Red rubbed his eyes. "I think I'm going to have to come mow it."

"You don't have to do anything! It's fine as is." Naturally it wasn't, but Myrtle didn't want Red hanging around her house more often than he already was.

"It reflects poorly on me, Mama. You live right across the street from me. It's not as if I don't know what kind of shape it's in. There could be vermin in there for all we know. Or the weeds and grass could wrap themselves around your leg and pull you down."

Myrtle fixed him with a withering stare. "Red Clover, I've survived eight decades on this planet without ever being tackled by my own lawn. I believe I can manage a few more weeks."

But Red's expression seemed to suggest the argument was over. He was going to do what he wanted, whether or not he admitted that fact to his mother. He said mildly, "Well, you'd better run along and get ready. Hope the two of you enjoy the party."

Now, however, Myrtle wasn't feeling in the most festive mood. Her eyes narrowed as she watched Red head back home.

Chapter Three

Miles said, "Come on, Myrtle. It's time for us to meet Wanda over there."

"You sound almost eager to attend Victoria's party."

Miles shook his head. "I'm eager to get it over with."

So Myrtle headed for her room and donned the funeral gear in her closet. It did in fact look rather funereal, which was naturally the point for its usual purpose. She put on a festive multi-colored beaded necklace and called her preparations done. "Let's go," she said as she walked back to join Miles in the living room.

Minutes later, they arrived at Victoria's. The restored Victorian mansion gleamed with fresh paint and new money. Its wraparound porches and ornate trim made it look like a Southern belle who'd undergone extensive cosmetic surgery.

Myrtle sniffed as she glanced around the grounds on her way in. "It's all very annoying how Dusty does such a fabulous job for anybody willing to give him a little money."

"I suspect Victoria is giving him a *lot* of money," said Miles.

"Buying his loyalty. She's poached my yardman."

Miles said, "If we want to stay at this party and not be escorted out, you'd probably better keep those sentiments under your hat."

They walked in to find a small number of people. Such a small number of people that Myrtle blinked. Tippy Chambers, Myrtle's friend from garden club, book club, and a host of other activities, gave her a smile. Myrtle smiled quickly in return.

Miles shifted uncomfortably. "Myrtle," he said under his breath. "There aren't even ten people here."

"Well, who on earth sends out engraved invitations for a minor event?" hissed Myrtle.

"Rich people."

Myrtle said, "Actually, this makes it even more important that we're here. Wanda would likely have been even *more* uncomfortable in a small group."

Miles didn't appear to think this was the case. He grumbled softly as they headed for their hostess. Victoria was a well-preserved woman in her mid-forties with what were probably expensive honey-blond highlights. She was tall and striking in silk and cashmere. She had the sort of predatory charm that made small-town people feel both flattered and vaguely uneasy, like being complimented by a beautifully-dressed cobra.

Victoria bared her perfect teeth in a smile as Myrtle and Miles approached. "Miss Myrtle," she said. "What a pleasure to have you here tonight. Everyone says you were always one of their favorite teachers."

Myrtle preferred to be *the* favorite teacher, but at least Victoria had started off with a compliment. "Thank you, my dear.

That's very kind of you. Remind me where you grew up, again? And when you moved to Bradley."

"Atlanta," she said with a rueful smile, perhaps knowing that Bradley residents viewed the large city and its accompanying traffic with horror. "I've been here two years now."

"Ah, I see. Miles moved here from Atlanta," said Myrtle.

Victoria turned her smile on Miles, who became rather red at the attention. "I think I've seen you around town," she added huskily. "You've very distinguished-looking."

With some difficulty, Myrtle kept from rolling her eyes.

Miles opened his mouth, but what came out was indecipherable.

Victoria charitably overlooked this. "I'm delighted to have you both attend my little séance. Would you like a tour of the house? I'm just about to give one."

They nodded and trailed along behind Victoria with the rest of the guests falling in line for the tour.

Wanda gave Myrtle and Miles a subdued greeting. She already looked a bit stressed, with lines pronounced around her eyes and mouth. "Gud to see you."

Myrtle said, "And I you. I do hate to alarm you, but Victoria seems to still be expecting a séance."

"Dun told her I don't do 'em. The spirits don't wanna be bothered."

Myrtle nodded at this. "Well, naturally they don't. It's like pulling someone out of a deep sleep, isn't it?"

Miles looked even more uneasy than he already had been. "Wanda, what are you going to do? Victoria looks to be bulldozing you into this. You won't walk out in protest or anything, will you?" He looked anxious at the idea.

Wanda shook her head. "It'll be okay. Jest watch."

She loped along behind the other guests, with Myrtle and Miles taking up the rear of the tour.

"At least Tippy and Benton are here," said Miles dolefully. "It's good to see some familiar faces."

"All the faces are familiar to me. But then, I've been here all my life."

They grew quiet as the group halted for Victoria's first stop on the tour. "I want to officially welcome you all to Wisteria Hall. This conservatory is one of my favorite spots in the house."

The conservatory was quite humid, and Myrtle felt her poofy hair deflate a bit in response. The room was filled with the vibrant colors of summer's last hurrah. Myrtle spotted chrysanthemums, purple asters, ginger lilies and spider lilies, and roses.

"How magnificent," said Tippy. Myrtle detected a note of envy in her voice.

Victoria strode further ahead, pointing out the grand staircase. "Isn't this amazing? Wisteria Hall was built in 1878 by the Monroe family. Of course, we have Adelaide Monroe, a descendent and my neighbor, here with us today."

Victoria started applauding, and the other guests dutifully joined in.

Adelaide gave a tight smile but didn't speak.

Victoria continued in a prompting manner. "Adelaide, how wonderful that you're here to share your family's history with us."

"Some history is better left undisturbed." Adelaide's voice was flat.

"Oh, I'm not so sure about that," trilled Victoria, leading the group toward the dining room. "We must embrace the past to move forward, mustn't we? Now take a look at the dining room. I've restored every detail to its original splendor. Note the crown molding, the hand-painted wallpaper, and the servants' passages."

"Servants' passages?" Tippy looked intrigued despite herself. It did have a very *Downton Abbey* feel to it.

"Wisteria Hall is jampacked with hidden doorways and concealed staircases. Isn't that fun? The spirits during the séance will have so many ways to make their presence known."

Miles gave Wanda a meaningful look, but she carefully kept her gaze trained away.

The tour took them up the grand staircase to the second floor, meandering through what seemed like a vast number of bedrooms and sitting rooms with large pieces of very dark furniture and old oriental rugs.

Myrtle wished she still had her tennis shoes on. She'd had no idea she was going to be walking so far at a party.

Finally, the tour ended. Victoria said, "Now we'll head back to the conservatory for some food and beverages. I decided that would be a more intimate environment than the dining room would offer."

When the group arrived back at the conservatory, they found that a table and chairs had magically appeared, along with paraphernalia that were Wanda's stock in trade: a crystal ball, tarot cards, and other odds and ends. Myrtle suspected there must be a full, discreet staff running everything in the background.

The outdoors was suddenly lit up for a couple of seconds, followed almost immediately by a crashing boom. The guests all jumped.

Victoria grinned. "I couldn't have planned this better myself. The storm really sets the stage, doesn't it?"

Wanda settled herself quietly at the table. Victoria frowned. "Wanda, I think we'll let everyone serve themselves from the buffet first. We're keeping it casual tonight. We'll eat before the séance commences." Victoria pointed out that she had personalized teacups at each seat, which would serve as place cards. "Consider them party favors to take home. A little memento."

The food was catered from a place out of town. Victoria's idea of casual included carved beef tenderloin, cedar plank salmon, truffle mac and cheese that probably cost more than Myrtle's electric bill, and vegetables arranged so artfully they looked like they belonged in a magazine rather than on a plate. Some guests lined up immediately at the buffet while others chatted in groups to wait.

Myrtle noticed Walter Beaumont hovering near Victoria at the buffet table, clearly trying to catch her attention. Victoria glanced his way, then immediately struck up a conversation with Adelaide Monroe, her back to Walter.

Wanda could usually eat anyone under the table, but had helped herself to a tiny bit of the mac and cheese, which she proceeded to push around on her plate.

"What's going on?" asked Myrtle under her breath.

Wanda just shook her head at her. "Bad vibes."

"You're not just worried about doing readings instead of a séance? Because I don't think it's that big of a deal. Victoria will simply have to accept it."

Wanda shook her head again and continued pushing the pasta.

Myrtle was seated between Wanda and Tippy. Miles was looking miserable far away at the large, round table, seated between two people he didn't know.

Although Wanda wasn't saying a word, Tippy was quite animated. "Myrtle, how is everything going? I feel like I haven't spoken to you for ages."

"It's been okay. I'm having some issues with my yardman." Myrtle glowered at Victoria, who was sipping her tea and not looking her way.

"Gracious. You're using Dusty, aren't you? I hope he hasn't been under the weather." Tippy was naturally too well-bred to say anything negative about the state of Myrtle's yard. But Myrtle was certain Tippy was aware of it. After all, Tippy was aware of pretty much everything in the town of Bradley.

"Dusty is decidedly not under the weather. He's spending all his time here at Wisteria Hall, beautifying the already-beautiful grounds."

Victoria, who was sitting on the other side of Tippy, did hear a snippet of this. "Oh, do you use Dusty, too, Miss Myrtle? Isn't he amazing?"

"He's something else, all right." Myrtle stabbed her tenderloin rather viciously with her fork.

Victoria continued, "You'd never think that he had such a vision with landscaping."

"No, you'd never think that," agreed Myrtle.

"He's completely self-taught, you know."

Myrtle said, "That I can imagine."

Victoria and Tippy started talking about their own elaborate gardens. Wanda was still morosely abusing her truffle mac and cheese. Myrtle decided to just eat and observe what might go on at the table.

"Mason, you simply must tell everyone about that crown molding detail in the library," Victoria called across the table, her voice a touch too bright. Mason's jaw tightened slightly, but he gave a brief nod before immediately turning back to his conversation with Benton about permits.

Conversations buzzed around her. Mason Thornhill was regaling Walter Beaumont, owner of the local inn, with the details of the renovation work his company had spearheaded. Walter was looking quite deflated as he glanced around Wisteria Hall. Meanwhile, Ellie Thornhill deftly inserted herself into Victoria and Tippy's chat to admire the teacup artistry while casually reminding everyone she was a potter.

Myrtle's ears also pricked up when she overheard Victoria telling Benton, "I'll need to speak with you and Tippy again soon about the permits and the zoning issues for Wisteria Hall. We really need to get that taken care of. Also, I've noticed some local code violations going on. We don't allow livestock in the town limits, surely."

Benton drawled, "I'm not aware of such a code. This area was quite rural at one time, you know."

"Perhaps there should be a review of the zoning codes, then. Considering times have changed. I'm certain I saw a rooster wandering around a front yard when I was driving into town yesterday."

Benton hurriedly agreed to look up any pertinent zoning codes, although it was his wife, Tippy's, area at town hall. Myrtle pressed her lips together. Perhaps Scotty's stay at Elaine's house was going to be a short one.

When the meal wrapped up, the caterers, who'd been quietly working in the background, came to the forefront. They cleared the plates and poured wine. Victoria stood to walk over to Wanda's spot at the table. "We are about ready to begin," Victoria asked, a touch of impatience in her voice.

Wanda cleared her throat, looking earnestly at Victoria. "We cain't do the séance."

Victoria's expression was thunderous. "What on earth do you mean? Of *course* we can."

Wanda shook her head. "It's no gud. Bad things will happen. Spirits here ain't happy."

Victoria gave a short laugh. "You've got to be kidding me. I've specifically invited everyone to attend a séance. They're expecting to contact the beyond."

"The spirits don't want it. Don't wanna be entertainment. Let's do readin's instead."

Myrtle swiftly stepped in. "Honestly, Victoria, personal readings are far more interesting than séances. Who wants to hear from some random dead person when you could learn something about your own life?"

Victoria's chin jutted out ominously. But then Tippy, who had a sort of sixth sense for peacemaking, chimed in with practiced diplomacy. "Oh, readings! How fun! Benton and I were just saying we'd love to have our palms read, weren't we?" She nudged her husband, Benton, who looked both startled and trapped.

Wanda's relief was palpable. Victoria clearly wanted to argue but was being socially outmaneuvered. Myrtle was certain the only psychic phenomenon Benton had ever discussed was his ability to predict the stock market.

With that settled, everyone sipped their wine while Wanda cleared her throat and shyly introduced herself. "Reckon our hostess should go first. As a thank yew."

Everyone heartily agreed with this. Victoria smiled that toothy grin and held out her hand to Wanda. Wanda gingerly took it. Then her eyes opened wide, and she dropped Victoria's hand as if it had burned her.

Which was when the thunderstorm began raging again outside and wind gusts drove rain at the windows.

And the lights went out.

Chapter Four

There were gasps in the room, both delighted and exasperated. Victoria's voice was tight as she said, "Sorry, everyone. I'll find us some candles and flashlights."

The room was illuminated at intervals when lightning streaked across the window. Which was to say it wasn't lit much at all. There were only brief impressions of the people around the table, some standing, some sitting.

Benton was grumbling. "Never should have come. What a night. Now we can't even see to get out of here and head back home."

Tippy shushed him. "Victoria's finding candles and flashlights. Everything will be just fine."

A few moments later, Victoria returned. As the lightning streaked by again, she laid a bag on the table. "Flashlights, candles, and a lighter. Please, everyone, help yourselves." She paused, swaying slightly. "I need to check that the storm isn't impacting some of the more recent renovations. I'll be back soon."

Mason, the contractor, rose. "Should I go instead?"

"No, no. Stay. You're not supposed to be working tonight. I'll let you know if anything's wrong." Victoria swayed slightly again and put out a hand to the table to steady herself.

Victoria's voice sounded rather odd to Myrtle's ears. Tippy said solicitously, "Are you all right, Victoria? You sound breathless."

"I'm fine," said Victoria tersely before she made her way out the conservatory door. "Just warm." Victoria wiped some perspiration from her forehead.

Miles retrieved the bag and carefully set up the candles. Their flickering light cast odd shadows around the room, making it look far spookier than it had before.

Tippy cleared her throat. "Should we wait for Victoria? Or continue with the readings?"

Benton growled, "I think it's time for all of us to head back home. This storm is pretty bad. We'll need to drive slowly."

"Past your bedtime, Benton?" asked Mason lightly.

Benton didn't deign to answer.

Wanda looked uncertain. Not just uncertain. Myrtle frowned. Wanda looked almost fearful.

Tippy clearly noticed Wanda's expression. She likely also felt the tension in the room and decided she'd create a distraction. "How about if you read my palm?" she asked Wanda, thrusting it toward her.

Wanda gently took her hand. She didn't drop Tippy's, as she had Victoria's. She held it closer to the candlelight. "Ah see yew've got a long lifeline," she started slowly.

Tippy smiled at her. "Well, that's a good thing. I do like hearing that."

Wanda smiled back, gaining enough confidence to continue with a fairly glowing view of Tippy's long future, involving travel, creative pursuits, and what sounded suspiciously like a prediction that Benton would learn to appreciate fine literature. Myrtle only hoped that *Tippy* would appreciate it, since the book club's monthly picks were most egregious in terms of literary merit.

The men seemed a little uncertain about the readings, so Myrtle volunteered to go next. But Wanda shook her head. "Reckon we shud look after Victoria."

"Good thinking," said Myrtle. "Surely she should have returned to her party by now."

Miles said, "She was checking on something. Perhaps that held her up."

"I'm with Wanda. Let's go find her," said Myrtle.

Benton demurred. "I'm going to stay put in my chair like a sensible person."

Mason quickly said, "I'll stick around with you, Benton. Victoria might come back and wonder where all her guests have gone."

"Good point," Walter agreed.

Adelaide added, "I don't trust my footing in the dark."

"We have flashlights," said Myrtle. She refrained from adding "you ninny" to the end of the sentence and mentally complimented herself.

Although they'd just gone on a tour of the mansion, none of them had obviously been taking notes. "Which way should we go?" asked Miles. Because Miles, being the gentleman he was, naturally escorted Tippy, Wanda, and Myrtle on their hunt for Victoria.

Tippy said, "Maybe after checking on the renovation, she wanted to check in with the caterers. Perhaps the catering staff was supposed to bring out desserts."

Miles looked uneasy. "Are we sure that 'checking on something' wasn't code for 'visiting the restroom?' It might be awkward to have a search party finding Victoria under those circumstances."

But Wanda looked more certain of where to go. "This way," she said, heading for the stairs.

"Clever Wanda," said Myrtle.

Wanda seemed to have an unerring sense of direction, leading them to the far end of the second-floor hallway. They were now in an area of the house that hadn't been on Victoria's tour.

Tippy, however, was clearly unsure about this. "Shouldn't we be searching somewhere else? Maybe we should find Victoria's bedroom. She didn't appear to be feeling well. She might have wanted to lie down."

Miles made an unhappy sound at the thought of searching out bedrooms for Victoria.

But Wanda kept loping toward a narrow staircase that was tucked away at the far end of an equally narrow corridor. There was a crash of thunder right on top of a jagged streak of lightning that lit up a small window.

Tippy and Miles hesitated. "Up there?" Miles asked as Wanda unerringly headed toward the staircase.

"Of course," said Myrtle. "Are you going to question the psychic?"

The four of them trudged up the stairs, Myrtle taking special care to lean on her cane. The staircase was an old one and hugged them on both sides as they ascended.

"Careful," said Wanda. "It done rained in."

Myrtle breathed, "We're going to the widow's walk on the roof."

Miles made another unhappy mutter, but at least Tippy seemed onboard with their expedition.

Wanda pushed open the door at the top of the stairs, but the door was already ajar and rain had blown through onto the staircase. The rain continued pelting down, with the lightning and thunder chiming together at once. And during one streak of lightning, they saw Victoria lying on the wooden floor of the widow's walk.

Chapter Five

Myrtle said, "Tippy, call Red."

Miles was already feeling for a pulse and, finding none, sat back on his heels, shaking his head. "She's gone." His voice was disbelieving.

Myrtle leaned on her cane, studying Victoria. There didn't seem to be any signs of a struggle. Nor were there any weapons or obvious wounds.

Tippy was speaking urgently with Red in the background before wrapping up the call. "He's on his way."

The rain was unrelenting; they were all completely soaked to the skin. Tippy shivered, and Miles said, "We should all go back inside." He hesitated. "It feels wrong to leave Victoria out here in the elements."

And the elements were getting worse every second. But Myrtle said, "We have to leave her. This is a crime scene. A very poor excuse for a crime scene. Let's go inside."

Miles said, "Remember, the stairs are slick. Watch your footing as we head downstairs."

It seemed to take a very long time for them to climb back down to the hallway. They were silent as they went, concentrating on keeping their balance, but also all thinking about Victoria on the roof in the storm.

Miles breathed a sigh of relief as they finally reached the hall. Tippy, always organized, said, "Should one or more of us wait here at the doorway? Just to make sure no one goes up to disturb the scene?"

Wanda bobbed her head. "I'll stay with yew."

Myrtle said, "And Miles and I will protect the other crime scene."

"What crime scene is that?" asked Miles with a frown.

"The conservatory. Victoria's tea was clearly poisoned."

They all gaped at Myrtle in the flashlight's glare. "Her tea?" repeated Tippy.

"Certainly. I don't think the catering staff poisoned the buffet. No, Victoria was targeted. The only way to do that was to tamper with her tea. Or, I suppose her wine, but a poison might have been more obvious in a wine glass. I'd think it would have clouded up the liquid, wouldn't it?"

"Look, we're all soaking wet," said Tippy. "There must be a linen closet somewhere nearby, considering all the bedrooms on this floor. We'll catch our death standing around like this."

She found one quickly and returned with an armful of plush towels. Miles and Myrtle patted themselves down as best as they could while Wanda, still shivering, wrapped one around her shoulders.

Myrtle strode toward the conservatory, her cane thumping as she went.

Miles hurried to catch up with her. "You think she's been murdered," he said under his breath.

"Absolutely. A woman Victoria's age doesn't have sudden onset of illness that results in her death just minutes later. It would be absurd."

Miles said, "Who would want to kill Victoria?"

"That's precisely what we're going to find out. And Miles, let's not mention Victoria's death to the others. I'd like to do a bit of prying before everyone shuts up. Although," said Myrtle thoughtfully, "the killer might shut up anyway. Knowing what they must."

"How are you planning on preserving the crime scene if everyone is still in there?"

Myrtle said, "I'll say we'll be more comfortable in the living room, of course. Which we will be. Those conservatory chairs were lovely antiques, but they certainly weren't designed for comfort."

"Won't we get them soaked?"

"We're dry enough," said Myrtle. "Besides, who's going to care now? Victoria is dead."

The group in the conservatory had become a bit more raucous. Myrtle and Miles could hear the laughter before they'd even reached the room. Myrtle was certain wine and boredom were to blame. The laughter died down as they walked through the door.

"Let's adjourn to the living room," said Myrtle. "I'm quite old and these stiff chairs aren't kind to me for long stretches."

Adelaide's face creased in concern. "Where's the psychic? And Tippy?" She was a sharp-eyed woman in her seventies with steel-gray hair pulled into a neat chignon. Adelaide was wearing, as usual, a practical cardigan and sensible shoes, although she'd put on what looked like very fine jewelry as a nod to the dressiness of the event.

"And where's Victoria, for that matter?" asked Walter Beaumont, looking concerned. "Didn't you find her?"

"Of course we found her," said Myrtle impatiently. "It wasn't as if she was going to run away from home when she was hosting a party. Victoria is feeling slightly unwell. Tippy and Wanda are staying with her to make sure she's all right. In the meantime, we're all heading to the living room. Now."

There was clearly no arguing with Myrtle. Obediently, they quietly followed her out of the room, clutching flashlights and candles as they went.

Red was obviously on his way, if not this very instant, then extremely soon. The only thing that would have delayed him was if he'd been helping with a road accident in the bad weather. Even then, he'd have handed off the accident to a deputy and come by. Murder trumped everything. She'd have to move fast before Red ruined her investigating, as he always did.

Myrtle turned to Adelaide first as the men started talking about their golf games, giving scores that sounded wildly exaggerated. Miles didn't seem inclined to join in, so was listening in on Myrtle's conversation with Adelaide. The older woman was jumpy-looking and clearly hadn't been drinking as much as the others, who were still clutching their wine glasses.

Adelaide had taught Latin at the high school when Myrtle had been teaching English. They'd always gotten along fine, although Myrtle wouldn't have termed them close. But as far as she could remember, Adelaide lived right next door. Naturally, as Victoria had mentioned, Wisteria Hall had formerly belonged to the Monroe family before hard times had resulted in their needing to sell it. "Adelaide, you're Victoria's neighbor, aren't you? Living in what used to be a gamekeeper's quarters, correct?"

Adelaide frowned vaguely at Myrtle's rather officious tone. "That's right. It's a very nice place." She sounded rather defensive, as if Myrtle had been intimating that the gamekeeper's quarters weren't nice at all.

Myrtle waved her hand in the air. "I'm sure it's just fine. I was just wondering what Victoria is like as a neighbor." She was very proud of herself for using the present tense.

Adelaide cast uneasy glances at the door as if certain Victoria was going to come barreling in at any moment. She quietly said, "Victoria? Well, I suppose she's just fine. We don't do very much together, of course. There's an age difference."

That was putting it mildly. Adelaide could be Victoria's grandmother. Myrtle said, "Naturally. I was just wondering. The grounds at Wisteria Hall are quite sprawling, aren't they? Didn't I hear that there were some boundary disputes in times past?"

Myrtle had heard no such thing, but would be quite surprised if there *hadn't* been boundary disputes. Victoria looked like the sort of person who could easily perpetuate a land grab.

Adelaide threw another nervous look at the door before saying in a quiet tone, "Really, Victoria's just *fine*, Myrtle."

This made Myrtle even more certain that Victoria wasn't. Miles gave her a quelling sort of look, but Myrtle ignored it.

"Actually, didn't I hear in garden club that you'd had some sort of damage done to your heritage garden? Didn't you have heirloom plants there?" asked Myrtle. She was sure she could hear the faint sound of a siren in the distance, accompanied by more peals of thunder.

This inquiry seemed to be the key to unlocking a torrent from Adelaide. "Heavens, yes. My poor garden. There were some amazing, amazing varieties of plants there that sustained *such* damage. They were flooded. You simply wouldn't believe it."

Adelaide said the last bit to Miles, who apparently looked more sympathetic and less like he was pumping for information Adelaide didn't want to provide. Miles gave her a kind smile, and she beamed gratefully at him.

Myrtle gave Miles a meaningful look, and he cleared his throat, prepared to take over the questioning, but gently. "The garden sounds like it must have been very old. Heirloom plants?"

"That's right. All sorts. Most of them were originally from Wisteria Hall, from when my family owned the mansion. Of course, they sold it a generation ago when the cost of maintaining it all grew too much."

Myrtle gave Miles another meaningful look. He said in an almost apologetic tone, "What caused the flooding, Adelaide? Aside from the storm tonight, I don't remember us getting too much heavy rain lately."

"We haven't," said Adelaide. After casting another look at the door, she said in an undertone, "It was Victoria's new landscaping. The rain we got plus her landscaping was enough to flood my historic boathouse and damage the garden. I'm sure that's why Victoria invited me here tonight. She wanted to make things up to me."

Myrtle raised her eyebrows. "Surely the best way to make it up to you was by offering you remuneration of some kind. Not by inviting you to a party."

Adelaide pursed her lips before saying, "Well, different people have different ways of making amends."

Still, there seemed to Myrtle that there was something Adelaide wasn't sharing with her. While she was mulling over what this might be, Adelaide asked, "I'm a little surprised to see you here, Myrtle. And Miles." She blushed a bit as her gaze flickered shyly over to Miles.

Miles flushed.

Myrtle said, "You're right that Miles and I aren't close friends with Victoria. Perhaps she was looking for an eclectic group of people for her party. I'd imagine folks who entertain a lot enjoy having guests who are very different. Also, Miles and I are good friends of Wanda's."

Adelaide frowned as if she couldn't quite remember who Wanda was.

"The psychic," said Myrtle.

"Oh, right, right. Of course. Goodness, what an unusual skill to have."

The siren came closer, and Adelaide tilted her head with a frown.

Myrtle quickly said in a low voice, "I thought I'd seen guests tonight casting hard looks at our hostess. Do you know of any bad feelings between Victoria and anyone?"

Adelaide looked surprised, as if she hadn't considered Myrtle to be a gossip. "You must be talking about Walter Beaumont," she said in an equally low voice. "I must confess I was surprised to see him here tonight. I supposed Victoria was trying to make up with him or something."

"Make up with him? Had she done something *to* him?"

Adelaide glanced over at Walter to make sure he wasn't listening in. But he was having a fine time talking with Mason and Benton. And drinking the rest of his beverage. "Walter has been complaining about Victoria poaching the staff from his hotel."

Myrtle frowned. "Why would she do that? This is a private home."

"Oh, didn't you know?" Adelaide looked delighted at having a tidbit that Myrtle wasn't aware of. "Victoria is about to turn Wisteria Hall into a bed-and-breakfast. That's why she's been doing all the renovations and upgrading the landscaping. She wants it to be a major draw for the area."

"And Walter presumably isn't happy about that, considering the fact that he owns Bradley's only lodging."

"That's right," said Adelaide eagerly. "He sees it as major competition. And, of course, it hasn't helped that Victoria has been offering his staff higher pay to come work here."

"Mercy," said Myrtle absently. Then she added, as subtly as she could, "When the lights went out and the storm became so wild, did you see anything?"

"See anything?" Adelaide looked confused. "What sort of thing?"

"Oh, I don't know. Someone leaning over Victoria's teacup?"

Adelaide blinked at this as if Myrtle had lost the use of her mind.

Myrtle considered this. Would the poison have had enough time to take effect if it was right when the power went out? Perhaps it made more sense if someone had poisoned her cup while people were at the buffet line. "Actually, did you see someone leaning over Victoria's cup at *any* time?"

Adelaide shook her head. "No. But then, I've been focused on myself, I'm afraid. I've felt a little out of place tonight. That sounds very self-absorbed of me, but it's the truth. I've been too nervous about how other people are viewing me than what other people are *doing*, if that makes sense."

It made sense, but it was regrettable.

Also regrettable was the fact she could hear Red's voice calling out, "Police!"

Everyone turned to look at Myrtle. She pressed her lips together. "I'll go talk to Red."

But before she could even rise out of her chair, Red was there, sopping wet from the rain, and holding a flashlight. He peered into the salon, training his light briefly on everyone before stopping at Myrtle.

"Mama!" he said, as if he blamed her for all of it.

"Let's go for a little walk," she said to him, rising and heading out to the hall. She could hear the others wondering what was going wrong and supposed Miles would finally fill them in, considering the proverbial cat was out of the bag with the arrival of the chief of police.

"What have you been up to?" Red muttered furiously as they headed toward the narrow staircase at the end of the hall.

"For heaven's sake. I haven't done *anything* except attend a party. Honestly, it was a rather dull party until the power went out and poor Victoria died."

Red said, "Yes, that's what I want to hear more about. How does a middle-aged woman suddenly die in the middle of a party? Did she fall? Did she seem to have a heart attack? An aneurysm?"

"She seemed to be poisoned," said Myrtle simply.

"*Seemed* to be? What does that even mean?" Red's voice rose. "Did you taste-test her tea?"

Myrtle didn't deign to answer, merely rolled her eyes. He'd find out she was right soon enough.

Chapter Six

They finally reached the spot where Wanda and Tippy were waiting for them. Tippy had seemed to chat lightly and with great determination to Wanda before their appearance. But then, it was in Tippy's nature to take over the hostess duties, under the circumstances. She looked rather relieved to see Red. "Wanda and I made sure no one went up those stairs," she said, gesturing to the door leading to the stairway.

Red opened the door and started up the narrow, steep stairs. No one made a move to join him.

Wanda had her towel wrapped around herself and was shivering. It wasn't obvious whether it was from the cool air, her still-wet clothing, or from Victoria's death.

Myrtle said, "Wanda, why don't you go downstairs? Everyone is sitting in that big living room."

"The salon," corrected Tippy in a vague voice.

"Whatever. That's where everyone is. Join up with Miles. He'll be vastly relieved that he doesn't have to be hanging out with all those folks he doesn't know."

Wanda nodded, then headed in that direction.

"How's it all going down there?" asked Tippy. "I can imagine everyone is in a state of shock."

"Actually, they're not at all shocked. Miles and I didn't disclose what happened. I figured I could perhaps get more information out of everyone that way. While everyone was off-guard, you see."

Tippy frowned. "The other guests don't know what happened to Victoria?"

"Well, they probably do *now*. They all seemed rather startled when Red came bursting in. Miles likely filled them in." Myrtle paused. Perhaps this was a good time to find out what Tippy might know. "Did you know Victoria very well?"

"Hmm?" asked Tippy, looking uncharacteristically distracted. "Oh. No, I wouldn't say I knew her *well*. I was hoping to get her to come to garden club tomorrow at my house. Her grounds are so beautiful that I figured it might be a hobby of hers."

"Did you ask her?"

Tippy nodded. "Yes. But then she told me she really had no interest at all in plants."

Myrtle frowned. "But her conservatory. A lack of interest in gardening seems hard to believe."

"That's what I thought, too. Then Victoria explained that she has a horticulturist she used to decorate the conservatory. That's the word she used: decorate." Tippy seemed quite bemused by this.

"How about Benton? Did he know Victoria well?" Myrtle wasn't sure what made her ask that question. Victoria had mentioned Benton and Tippy were to help her with permits and zoning.

Tippy hesitated before saying, "We've both spoken with Victoria a few times about zoning and permit issues. Did you know she was planning on turning Wisteria Hall into a bed-and-breakfast?"

"I did, yes." Although apparently far later than everyone else in town. "Was Victoria having a hard time getting business zoning for the house? I suppose it would require a permit since it's in a residential zone?"

"Yes. She'd also have to get approval for her signage, commercial food service regulations, and parking requirements."

Myrtle often forgot that Tippy was an elected official and served on the town council. Benton, of course, had gobs of political experience in Bradley. He'd served on the council several times and had been the mayor in the past. But now he was the chair of the planning and zoning commission. "And Victoria would have to get the support of both you and Benton to get the bed-and-breakfast off the ground."

Tippy appeared to be unhappy with the direction the conversation was heading. "I suppose so. She'd need my backing and Benton for the technical approvals."

She seemed very relieved when Red pulled the door open. "Let's get back downstairs," he snapped.

They quietly walked down the hall toward the grand staircase to descend to the ground level. Myrtle moved to start down the staircase, but Red said, "Nope. Me first. If you fall, just fall on me."

They made it down the flight in terse silence. Even Tippy, whose one desire was always to smooth everything over, was quiet.

Red strung crime scene tape at the bottom of the staircase when they'd finally descended.

"Were you able to protect the scene for forensics?" asked Myrtle.

Red glowered at his mother, as he usually did when she demonstrated an inordinate interest in crime. "As best I could. There's not much I can do in that kind of weather."

"A little tent?" suggested Myrtle.

"It would blow clean off the house in two seconds. I put a weighed tarp down, but I'm not sure that's going to suffice. And I took pictures, of course. Now, Mama, let's have a little chat about what happened tonight."

Myrtle let Tippy go first. She decided perhaps she might learn more from Tippy's perspective. Also, Tippy had a more soothing effect on her son than Myrtle did. She didn't need Red to storm away before she could elicit some information from him.

Tippy, happily, was fine with stepping into the role of informant. "Well, Wanda was starting out with the readings. Then the lights went out."

Red nodded. "Okay. Where was everyone?"

"We were all in the conservatory. That's where we ate dinner and where Wanda was doing the readings."

Red asked, "What was Victoria's mood like?"

Tippy considered this. "She seemed excited to be a hostess. She'd given us all a tour of Wisteria Hall and acted like she was pleased to tell us about its history and furnishings."

"She was feeling well, then?"

Tippy frowned at this question. "Victoria *had* been feeling well. At least, we hadn't heard anything to the contrary until later on. She seemed a little off before she walked out of the room. Her breathing was kind of labored, and she was perspiring."

Red said, "Okay. So she started feeling unwell. What made her leave the conservatory?"

"Candles and flashlights. She wanted to provide them for us. The lights had gone out at that point, so she was looking after her guests." Tippy thought a bit more. "Oh, and Victoria wanted to check on something."

Red raised his eyebrows. "Check on what?"

"She mentioned making sure the rain wasn't creating a problem with her renovations. I'd wondered if that was an excuse to monitor the catering staff. No desserts had been served yet, which I figured must be an oversight. Victoria had been so careful about everything else. But I guess it must not have been, since she was up on the roof."

Red seemed less interested in whether Victoria had planned the food well. "So the food was catered?"

"That's right. And the staff is still here."

Red's face fell at the prospect of having to interview the catering staff in addition to the party guests. "Okay. So now we're assuming, of course, that Victoria didn't go to the kitchen to ask about desserts. Because she was found on the roof."

"It's a widow's walk," said Myrtle helpfully.

Red glowered at her before continuing. "Do we know why she ended up on this widow's walk? Was she up there planning on meeting someone?"

"In a thunderstorm?" chided Myrtle.

"Was anyone missing in the conservatory?" asked Red between clenched teeth.

Tippy looked at Myrtle. "I don't think so. Do you know, Myrtle?"

"Everyone was at the table in the conservatory when the power went out. The guests are Walter Beaumont, Benton and Tippy, Adelaide Monroe, and Mason and Ellie Thornhill. Victoria left to get the candles and flashlights, returned with them, then went off to check on the renovations. She'd want to make sure the house hadn't sprung a leak, wouldn't she?"

Red gave a reluctant nod of agreement. "Although it seems weird she didn't have Mason Thornhill do it. Wasn't he the contractor in charge of the project?"

"Mason offered to check on any damage, but Victoria told him he was a guest and not working tonight." Myrtle added, "Also, the widow's walk was the sort of isolated spot where someone feeling disoriented from poison might seek fresh air."

Red scowled. "You just pointed out Victoria wouldn't have sought out that spot in a thunderstorm. That she was just making sure the rain wasn't causing any damage."

Myrtle shrugged. "Well, they could both be true. Victoria likely wasn't thinking clearly if she was poisoned."

Red rubbed his temples as if they were hurting. "That's the third time you've mentioned poison. Why do you have such a bee in your bonnet about that?"

"Because it's what makes the most sense, Red. Victoria was fine. She was at the top of her game and enjoying playing chatelaine of her chateau. A few sips of tea later, she wasn't feeling well, wandered off, and died on the widow's walk. Poison seems the most likely scenario."

Tippy picked up the story. "After Victoria didn't come back, we decided to check on her."

"Who was 'we'?" asked Red.

"Myrtle, Wanda, Miles, and me," said Tippy. "We formed a sort of search party."

Red sighed but looked as if he'd fully expected his mother would make an appearance at some point. "And you found her."

"We did," said Tippy, looking more cheerful at this part of the story. A part where she had done well. Perhaps the part where she felt a bit more in charge of the evening, right before things had gone horribly wrong.

Red tilted his head to the side inquiringly. "I'd like to know why y'all decided to go on the roof. I mean, if it was me, I believe I'd try the kitchen first. Or maybe see if Victoria had taken ill in her room."

Tippy's face fell. "Well, yes. Yes, that's true. I did think that, as I mentioned before."

Red looked between Tippy and his mother. "Soooo what made y'all go up on the roof, then."

"Because Victoria was there," said Myrtle in an irritated voice, as if Red failed to see the point.

Red rolled his eyes. "Mama, what I'm looking to find out is why you thought Victoria might be up on the roof."

"It's really a widow's walk, Red. An architectural feature."

Red said, "We're not doing a crossword here. What were you doing up there? I can't imagine you opened every door and went through every passage in this house before deciding to go up there. It's a big place."

Myrtle sighed as if she really couldn't stand another second of her son's inanity. "Because Wanda was with us, as Tippy mentioned. And since we had a psychic with us, we were spared having to open every door in the mansion."

Red's eyes narrowed. "So Wanda knew she was up there."

"For heaven's sake, Red! Wanda was with us the entire time in the conservatory. Most of the time, she was the focal point, in fact. You know how people are when they're around Wanda."

"No, I really don't," said Red. "How are they?"

"Stupefied! Amazed by her abilities. Curious. All of those things. Their gaze was always on Wanda."

Red said, "Until the lights went out."

"I can't stand this nonsense a moment longer. Here's what happened, Red: Victoria drank something poisonous, most likely in her tea, but maybe in her wine. It was most unlikely that it was in her food because there was less opportunity to compromise her food. The tea was sitting on the table in the conservatory while everyone was waiting to get their food from the buffet."

Red looked skeptical, so Myrtle huffed and continued. It was most aggravating that he wasn't connecting the dots. "Victoria drank the poisoned tea. The storm, which was out of everyone's control, knocked out the power. Victoria left for flashlights, returned with the flashlights and candles, then proceeded to go to the widow's walk to check how it was faring in the storm. That's what happened. *You* seem to think that Victoria left to either meet someone on the widow's walk or that she was followed by someone and murdered up there. That just didn't happen, I can promise you that."

Red now looked even more annoyed than he had before. "All right, point taken. Let's pick up at that part of the story."

Myrtle shrugged. "Tippy called you. Wanda and Tippy stayed near the door to the stairs to keep anyone from tampering with the scene. Miles and I headed back to the conservatory to preserve the crime scene there. Because *that* was the crime scene. We asked everyone to move to the living room instead."

Tippy carefully refrained from correcting her with 'the salon' that time.

Red's eyes narrowed again. "You asked everyone to go to the living room? That seems very helpful, Mama."

"I'm generally a helpful and responsible member of the community."

Red said, "And a nosy one. I don't suppose you questioned anybody at the party in the interim."

"Certainly not," said Myrtle with a sniff. "I simply made small talk. We were at a party, after all."

At that moment, there was a good deal of noise from the direction of the door.

"That'll be the state police," said Red.

"Oh good. I'd like to see Lieutenant Perkins."

Red said, "I don't know if Perkins is on duty."

But Perkins was on duty. Myrtle had gotten to know the policeman during a spate of murders in quiet Bradley, North Carolina. They had developed something of a friendship.

Red said, "Wait here." Then he was hurrying away from Tippy and Myrtle and toward the noise of the team that had arrived.

Myrtle trailed along behind her son as Tippy lingered obediently.

Several men, including Perkins, talked with Red. He appeared to be filling them in on what had occurred, pointing out the group in the living room, explaining there was catering staff on the premises, then directing them upstairs to the stairs leading to the widow's walk.

"Yoo-hoo!" said Myrtle. "Lieutenant Perkins!"

Red looked very displeased but not surprised that his mother hadn't stayed where he'd asked her to. He stomped off toward the others.

Perkins gave her a smile. "Mrs. Clover! It's a treat to see you again. Although I'm sorry for the circumstances."

Myrtle was very fond of Perkins. He was always such a gentleman. She also approved of the way he seemed to take care of his mother. Red was always so very exasperated with Myrtle.

"The circumstances aren't the best, are they? You and I should have dinner together at some point at my house."

Perkins gracefully side-stepped this idea with a quick change of subject. "How is Miles doing?"

"Oh, he's here tonight. He's in the living room with the other guests. And Wanda, you see."

Now Perkins looked a smidge startled. Perhaps he hadn't imagined that Wanda would be present at a party in a mansion. But he would naturally be too polite to state that outright. "Well, that's very nice, isn't it? Having your friends with you for the party, I mean."

"Yes, it was. Until the hostess was murdered. Sadly, Red doesn't seem to grasp how Victoria perished, but I'm sure you will." She quickly filled Perkins in. He paid very close attention to every word, jotting down notes from time to time on a small notepad he pulled from his jacket pocket.

At the end of this retelling, Perkins nodded. "I see what you mean. We'll make sure forensics does an analysis on that teacup and the wine glass, too. The team should be coming soon."

Myrtle frowned. "Actually, it just struck me that the state police arrived very quickly tonight. Especially considering there's a tremendous storm outside."

"It's the storm that put us in the area to begin with," he answered. "Police were deployed because of both road closures and a multi-car accident over on the highway. I was working nearby as duty supervisor from a command post."

"Mercy! I'd no idea that a storm was even coming."

Perkins said, "It sneaked up on all of us. The weather forecasters really dropped the ball on this one." He gave Myrtle a smile. "It's been lovely talking with you, and thanks for filling me in. I'll speak with Miles and Wanda so you can all be on your way. Make sure Miles drives slowly in this weather."

"Oh, I will. He's usually something of a speed demon, you know. He always has a lead foot on the accelerator." Or that was Myrtle's impression of Miles's sedate driving. On the way to the party, he'd seemed rather poky, of course.

Perkins was as good as his word. It wasn't long before Miles, Wanda, and Myrtle were free to leave. Miles looked more than ready, and Wanda seemed exhausted. So exhausted, in fact, that Miles was reluctant to have her drive at all, especially in a storm. Wanda was still an inexperienced driver.

Miles said, "Why don't you leave your car here, Wanda? We can come back for it tomorrow. I could drive you back to your house."

"What an excellent idea!" said Myrtle. "But there's no need for Miles to take you all the way home in this raging storm. Wanda, you may sleep in my guest room."

Wanda nodded wearily. "Sounds gud. Wud take me all night to git back home with the rain like this."

Miles, being Miles, carefully cleared with several policemen that they'd be temporarily leaving Wanda's vehicle on the Wisteria Hall grounds. Then they set off.

Chapter Seven

Although it wasn't a long drive, it took forever. The rain was still shooting out of the sky, and the roads were in poor shape. In some areas, it was a matter of large puddles. In other areas, it was a matter of the road being completely obscured by water.

"Turn around, don't drown," said Miles, which, naturally, he did. The number of flooded roads meant they had to take a very creative route back to Magnolia Lane. So creative that Myrtle had to put her thinking cap on to come up with long-forgotten shortcuts and cut-throughs. And Myrtle hadn't planned on using her thinking cap because she was still mulling over murder.

Finally, they reached Myrtle's house. From the car, they could see a sopping wet Pasha huddled on Myrtle's front porch.

"Pasha!" cried Myrtle. "Oh, the poor darling. I'd have left a window cracked for her if I'd known this ridiculous storm was coming. Drat those weather forecasters!"

"She's okay," said Miles mildly. "She's a feral cat, after all. I'd say Pasha is more prepared for this weather than we are."

Miles waited until Wanda and Myrtle had made it inside before he drove the short distance back to his own house.

Myrtle said, "We're all drenched. Even more than we were before, Wanda. Towels for us both."

A few minutes later, they had both dried off. Myrtle ran the heat, despite the warm humidity outside. "There's just something about getting rained on that makes me cold to the bones," she said. "Now, let me make sure the guest room is in order. That Puddin never cleans the way I want her to."

Fortunately, the guest room was unreproachable. Myrtle found a new toothbrush for Wanda, then pulled out one of her voluminous floral nightgowns. "It won't fit you," said Myrtle, "but perhaps it will do for tonight."

Then Myrtle insisted Wanda eat something. "I saw you pushing food around on your plate tonight. You can't go to sleep on an empty stomach. You'll wake up in the middle of the night hungry."

Myrtle found some pancake mix in her fridge and was lucky enough to have an egg and a bit of milk left. "I'll need to go to the store soon," she muttered.

By the time she'd finished making the pancakes, Wanda was snoring gently on the sofa, with Pasha curled up on her legs. Myrtle hated waking her up, but there was no way Wanda would sleep throughout the night in those circumstances: still wearing damp clothing and hungry. And on an old sofa instead of the bed in the guest room.

Wanda woke immediately and dove into the stack of pancakes as if she'd never eaten food before. Myrtle watched her friend with concern.

"You haven't eaten all day, have you?" she asked.

Wanda shook her head. "Nope. Too worried about that party."

Myrtle sighed. "I'm sorry. Sorry that you were put in that position by Victoria. And now, I suppose you won't even be paid."

"Don't matter. I'm sorry she's dead." Wanda took a sip of the milk Myrtle had brought her.

"You were worried about this party from the start. You knew something was going to happen, didn't you?"

Wanda nodded sadly. "Knew it, yeah. Wished she'd cancel. Asked her to. But she didn't."

"You thought someone would be murdered?"

"Nuthin' like that. Jest that somethin' bad wuz gonna happen. Didn't know whut."

Myrtle was quiet for a few moments. "When you started to read Victoria's palm, you dropped it quickly. What did you see?"

"Death," said Wanda grimly.

"That's it?"

Wanda nodded.

Myrtle said, "Okay. That must have been very alarming."

Wanda looked sad to remember it, so Myrtle felt she should move on. "Now, I know what the answer to this question usually is. But do you have any insights at all for me about this murder? Any clues at all?"

Wanda gave her a sad look. "The sight . . . "

"Yes, yes, I know. The sight doesn't work that way. Which is very unaccommodating of the sight."

Wanda was quiet for a few moments. "I do see somethin'. Cain't really explain it. Broken glass and old pictures."

"Well, that's most mysterious, Wanda. I hope you'll get some more clarity on that by and by."

Wanda tried to stifle a yawn, but Myrtle saw it. "Okay, let's get you off to bed. The guest room is set up for you. If you need anything, just ask me. I'll probably be awake for a while, processing everything."

Wanda sauntered off to bed with Pasha happily in tow.

Myrtle cleaned the kitchen, her mind racing the entire time. She wondered if she wrote a story quickly, whether her editor at the paper, Sloan Jones, would have the time to run it the next morning. It was getting close to midnight. She imagined it could *certainly* make the digital edition of the paper if not the paper one. She phoned him.

Sloan had been one of Myrtle's students in her high school English class back in the day. It was apparently an experience that he'd found very hard to shake. Whenever she phoned him, he reverted to being a teenager once again.

When he answered, Sloan sounded as if he'd been raised from a dead sleep. "Miz Clover! What's happening? What is it? Are you okay?"

"Why certainly I'm okay, Sloan. Why wouldn't I be? Are *you* okay? You don't sound like yourself." She paused. "Goodness. Were you asleep? I don't think of you as an early-to-bed early-to-rise enthusiast."

"Uh, no. I mean, yes, I was asleep. No, I usually don't turn in early."

Myrtle strongly suspected that Sloan had been out with his buddies at the local bar. That was his regular haunt. Considering the fact that he lived within walking distance of the establishment, he frequently appeared to visit it and walk home. Considering this, she supposed it was fairly amazing he'd wakened to her call.

"I wanted to let you know that Victoria Ashworth was murdered tonight," said Myrtle.

"What?"

Myrtle sighed. "Victoria Ashworth. She died at a party she hosted tonight. I was there. Since she's such an important figure in the community, I thought I'd write up a quick story for you to run in tomorrow's edition."

But Sloan seemed to find it hard to follow the conversation they were having. He repeated, "She's dead?"

"For heaven's sake, Sloan. Try to listen. Victoria hosted a party. She was murdered during the party. I'll quickly write an article for you to publish. That's it! I just need to know you'll stop the presses and slide this story in."

Sloan said slowly, "It doesn't really work that way, Miz Myrtle. We have a real small staff. The physical paper is already printed and bundled for delivery. There's no overnight printing staff here in Bradley. Those folks are already asleep."

"Gracious. Well, I guess you'll have to place an update in your subscriber newsletter then. And put it on social media, naturally."

"Naturally," said Sloan, sounding rather glum.

"I'll send it over to you in the next thirty minutes. You *will* be up, right?"

Sloan said sadly, "Oh, I'm wide awake now."

"Good." With that, Myrtle hung up and started working on her story.

Chapter Eight

Sometime later, the article and social media copy were sent to Sloan. Sometime even later than that, Myrtle was in her bed, staring up at the bunny-shaped crack on her ceiling in the nightlight's glow. It could be very difficult to sleep when one was thinking about murder. All things considered, it had been a most startling sort of evening. She'd originally thought that most of the drama would be limited to Wanda's desire not to hold a séance. But things had unraveled quite a bit more than she'd thought they would.

At some point, Myrtle drifted off to sleep. But she didn't stay in the arms of Morpheus for long. At around three-thirty, she got up, slung on her bathrobe, stuck her feet into a pair of slippers, and went into the living room. She felt like drinking a big cup of coffee, but didn't want to wake Wanda. She wondered if turning on the television would disturb Wanda's sleep at all, then decided perhaps she would chance it. It was too early for the newspaper delivery, so there wasn't a crossword to work on. Perhaps she could keep the volume down on the television. Myrtle had excellent hearing, a fact she was quite proud of.

A moment later, Pasha looked curiously around the corner of Wanda's room.

"Darling Pasha," crooned Myrtle. "Come to keep me company?"

Pasha had. She leaped up into Myrtle's lap, instantly curling up and falling asleep while Myrtle fiddled with the remote control, trying to find something worth watching. Sadly, the options between three and four a.m. were rather lacking. There was some sort of tacky infomercial, a football game that had apparently taken place in the distant past, news she certainly didn't feel like watching, and an animal show. She settled on the animal show.

It was about ten minutes later when Wanda surfaced. Myrtle gave her a guilty look. "I'm so sorry. Did I wake you up?"

Wanda shook her head. "Done slept like the dead until now. Reckon I got enuff sleep."

"Well, thank goodness for that. I always feel as if I'm in the position of waking everyone up. Ordinarily it's Miles, of course. I'm always calling him or going by his house and waking him up in the process. That man seems to sleep a good deal."

Pasha opened her eyes and transferred to Wanda's lap when Wanda sat on the sofa. Myrtle couldn't blame her. It always seemed as if Wanda and Pasha had a very comfortable relationship.

"Anythin' gud on?" Wanda asked, gesturing to the TV.

"Not at this godforsaken time of the night. The animal show is our best choice. I would play the tape of *Tomorrow's Promise*, but I wanted to save that for when Miles can join us." Myrtle glared at the wombats on the television screen. "For once, I'd like to see cute little lion cubs on the animal show. Is that too much to ask? Instead, I'm always bombarded with porcupines, wombats, and snakes. This show also seems to have a particular appreciation for marsupials. I simply cannot fathom it."

Wanda agreed mildly. They watched in companionable silence for several minutes as the wombats lived their lives. Pasha purred as Wanda gently rubbed her back. Myrtle rose at one point to make them both coffee and brought it in.

During a commercial break, Myrtle muted the TV and said, "Do you mind if I ask you about your impressions from last night? It somehow seems wrong for me to interrupt our peace and quiet with a discussion about murder."

"Nope, that's fine."

Myrtle said, "Okay, good. I can't seem to help myself from mulling over everything."

"It's whut yew do," said Wanda with a shrug.

"Right. So, thinking back to last night, I was wondering if anything stood out to you. I know you had a bad feeling about the evening very early on."

Wanda nodded. "Yep. Knew bad stuff was goin' down."

"Did those bad feelings seem to center on anyone in particular? Did you know Victoria was going to be a victim? Aside from when you held her hand for the reading, I mean."

Wanda considered this, then said, "No. Jest somethin' was gonna be bad."

"Got it. How about the other guests there? Did you pick up on anything malevolent about any of them? Did any seem particularly suspicious?"

Wanda shook her head regretfully. "That ain't the way the sight works."

"Well, let me ask this, then. Aside from the sight, did you get a bad feeling about any of the guests? I mean, just as a regular person." Which Wanda certainly wasn't. "Or can you provide any insight on the other guests?"

Wanda paused for a few moments, thinking. "That Mason man was pretty mad."

"Mad? I guess he was glowering at Victoria quite a bit. I wonder what that's about. Anything else?"

Wanda drawled, "Benton was nervous."

Myrtle thought back. Tippy's husband had indeed seemed rather uneasy about something. And she didn't think it had to do with being in a social situation. Tippy hosted dinners and other events all the time. "That's a good point," she said thoughtfully. "Maybe there's something going on there. Anything else?"

Wanda shook her head.

"Okay," said Myrtle as the commercial wrapped up. "So maybe I'll have the chance to speak with Mason and Benton soon. Of course, I really need to talk to *all* of the guests." She frowned. "Wait a minute. Today is garden club at Tippy's. Excellent. I can make the opportunity to talk to Tippy, at the very least. Maybe Benton will be there, too."

"At garden club?" asked Wanda, looking doubtful.

"You're probably right. Well, maybe he'll make an appearance. You'll come, won't you, Wanda? You know you like garden club. Tippy will have a tremendous spread of food and some punch. And you've liked the program in the past. You told me you've picked up some excellent tips for your own garden."

Wanda was quiet for a minute. Then she gave a small shake of her head. "Reckon I done had enuff social stuff."

Myrtle realized that, despite the sleep Wanda said she'd gotten, her friend still looked exhausted.

"Completely understandable," Myrtle said in a rush. "Of course you shouldn't attend. Perhaps Miles can drive you back to Wisteria Hall to get your car soon. I'll go along, too. Then maybe Miles would like going to garden club with me."

Wanda gave a gap-toothed grin. "Yew know he won't."

"No, but he can be persuaded," said Myrtle confidently.

It was some hours, a pot of coffee, and several nature shows later before Miles rang them up. The sun was rising in the sky.

"Is Wanda up?" he asked. "I thought I could drive her to get her car now."

"She's been awake for a while."

Miles said, "Did you sleep at all?"

"I basically took a nap after midnight and before three. How about you?"

Miles said, "I conked completely out. That whole ghastly evening exhausted me."

"Only parts of it were ghastly. Other bits weren't so very bad." She paused. "Why don't you come over for breakfast before we get the car? I'd like to get a meal into Wanda before she leaves. Or we can go to the diner."

Miles seemed to waffle on the other end of the line. "I guess eating at your house would be fine."

"What a rousing endorsement, Miles! You make it sound as if eating out of my kitchen is a last resort."

There was a bit of a pause. Then Miles said, "You do make a good breakfast."

"Why, thank you. I need to go to the store, though, at some point after I make it. I may have to get a bit creative with my offerings this morning. I didn't realize how low I was on food supplies."

Miles quickly said, "In that case, let's eat at the diner. I'll pay."

"You're rescinding your acceptance of my invitation? What on earth for?"

Miles said, "You and I have different ideas on cooking. When it starts becoming a creative endeavor, I back out."

"I'm certain that a chef would consider that a very short-sighted statement."

"I'm not a chef," said Miles. "And neither are you."

Wanda was watching Myrtle with a small smile on her face. She stroked Pasha, who lifted her head for Wanda to tickle her under her chin.

"Okay," said Myrtle with a sigh. "Let's go to the diner first. Then we'll pick up Wanda's car. Then you'll accompany me to garden club."

"How did garden club get tacked on?" Miles sounded startled.

"Because you don't appreciate my culinary creativity. The least you can do is take me to Tippy's for garden club."

Wanda grinned at her.

It was just minutes later when Myrtle, Miles, and Wanda were settled into a booth at Bo's Diner. It was a familiar spot for Myrtle, who'd been at the diner when she was a little girl, when the original Bo had been the owner. It was now owned by Bo's grandson, who was getting long in the tooth himself. There were vinyl booths, laminated menus, and a sign on the wall stating *The language you use in church is good enough to use in here.*

"What are we eating today?" asked their waitress, Candy, with a smile. She pointed a ballpoint pen at Miles. "Let me guess. Oatmeal."

Miles seemed somewhat abashed that he was that predictable. "That's right," he said sadly. Then he brightened. "But I'll have tea instead of coffee."

"Way to shake things up," said Candy approvingly. "And for you two ladies?"

Wanda ordered the country skillet and a coffee.

Myrtle said, "I'm feeling like the lumberjack special."

Candy grinned at her. "Honey, you always crack me up when you order that. I want to be you when I grow up."

Myrtle's eyes twinkled at her. This particular waitress never annoyed her, and it didn't even bother her when she called her honey or sweetie. That's because it was done out of fondness and not in infantilizing her like the others. "It's something to aspire to."

"The thing is, you clean your plate. And that's a lot of food. Good for you," said Candy. "Okay, I'm getting this order in. Y'all flag me down if you need anything else."

Miles glanced at the door as it opened. Then he frowned. "Uh-oh. It's Red."

"There's no uh-oh about it, Miles. We're allowed to hang out at a diner, even very early in the morning. As far as I'm aware,

Red is only exasperated with me because I found a body last night. I don't believe there are any bodies at Bo's Diner."

"At least not currently," said Miles morosely. "There have been before."

Myrtle turned, which was right when Red spotted them. He didn't look especially pleased to see the three of them.

Chapter Nine

"**C**ome sit with us," called out Myrtle. It was less of an invitation than a command.

"Not planning on staying," he said quickly. "I've gotta get it takeout."

"Then sit with us while you wait for it to be cooked. For heaven's sake, Red, act as if you like us."

Red walked reluctantly over to them after placing his order at the counter. "Well, if it isn't Nancy Drew and the gang."

Myrtle said, "I don't think we fit that analogy. If I'm Nancy, Miles would have to be Ned Nickerson. And Miles isn't my love interest."

Miles nodded his agreement of this.

"And Wanda would have to be Bess or George. She's not remotely like either one of them."

"Okay, okay, Mama. I get it." Red paused. "I was about to ask what you were doing up so early, which means I must have lost my mind."

"Indeed you have. I've been up since three-ish. To answer your question, we're all grabbing breakfast before driving Wanda to get her car at Wisteria Hall."

Red frowned. "It's all still blocked off there. Forensics got there pretty late because of the storm."

Wanda quickly said, "I done parked on the street. Didn't wanna take up parkin' the guests needed."

"Well then, you'll be able to get your vehicle. That was good foresight on your part," said Red.

"Wanda is all about foresight," pointed out Myrtle. "Being a psychic."

Red rubbed his forehead as if it hurt.

"Did you even go home last night?" asked Miles of Red.

"Yep, but not long enough. I grabbed an hour or two."

Myrtle would not let the opportunity to ask for information pass. "I'm assuming you found poison was the culprit."

"You know I don't talk about active investigations," said Red automatically. He looked over at the counter, hoping his to-go bag would magically appear.

"You're at least calling it murder, aren't you? You don't think that healthy young woman just dropped dead, do you?"

Red sighed. "We're treating it as a suspicious death. Look, even if I wanted to share information with you, which I don't, forensics hasn't finished with the evidence yet."

"Pooh on forensics," said Myrtle sourly.

"Well, it takes time to do stuff right." He narrowed his eyes. "And I don't want you involved at all in this investigation, do you understand? Whenever you start getting nosy, bad things happen."

"Bad things? Like solving cases?" asked Myrtle with a sniff.

Red cast another longing look at the counter and was rewarded this time as the waitress held up his takeout bag. He swiftly stood up. "Gotta run. Good seeing you, Miles and Wanda." He looked over at his mother, sighing again. "Talk to you later, Mama."

Myrtle watched as he quickly paid for his food and left the diner. "Red is most aggravating. Even more annoying is the fact I can't even get Dusty to put out my gnomes in retaliation."

"Sure 'bout that?" asked Wanda. "Reckon Dusty ain't gonna be workin' fer Victoria now."

"Gracious! You're right about that. I didn't even consider the ramifications of Victoria's death. I'll call Dusty before going to garden club."

Further conversation was temporarily and happily suspended by their food.

After they'd gotten Wanda back to her car, Miles dropped Myrtle at her house with glum assurances he'd pick her up for garden club shortly.

Myrtle set about calling Dusty. The phone rang and rang on Dusty's end before he finally picked it up with a howl. "Too hot to mow!"

"I can't even believe the nonsense coming out of your mouth, Dusty. It's not hot or cold or wet. The conditions are perfect for mowing. My yard is a disgrace. Even Red is talking about mowing it."

"Let 'im do it," said Dusty immediately.

"Certainly not. I don't want him anywhere near my house right now. Besides, his life is currently consumed with work. As you're about to find out, if you don't already know."

"I don't know nuthin'," said Dusty sullenly.

"That's painfully clear. I regret to inform you that Victoria Ashworth died at her home last night."

There was a long pause at the other end.

"Whut?"

"Victoria Ashworth. The woman whose yard you abandoned mine for. She perished at a party I attended last night."

Dusty gave a very heavy sigh and muttered something under his breath.

"What's that?" asked Myrtle.

"I said that seems kinda convenient. You were there, huh?"

"Are you saying *I* killed Victoria?"

Dusty grunted. "Seems like you might have been mad at her. Since I done been workin' in her yard, not yours."

"No, that made me mad at *you*, not at Victoria. And I'm going to continue being angry until you rectify the situation. I need the yard cut, pronto. I've got garden club today at Tippy's and having my yard look like a jungle makes me feel like a pretender. Following mowing, I need my garden gnomes pulled out."

"You're makin' a statement? Fer Red?" Dusty's voice was amused. "Whud he do now?"

"Everything. He's just an extremely annoying person. So be sure to pull out the entire battalion."

"Got it." Dusty's voice wasn't happy.

"I realize you're not pleased your golden goose is gone. But you made a fine living before. It'll be fine again soon."

Dusty snorted on the other end. "Not *as* fine."

"See you soon."

Myrtle ended up having to call Dusty twice more to motivate him to leave his house and come to hers. Finally, he showed up just as Miles pulled into her driveway to take her to Tippy's.

"You must be delighted that Dusty's back," said Miles as they headed to garden club.

"My yard was starting to make Erma Sherman's look good," said Myrtle with a shudder. "That simply couldn't be tolerated."

Unfortunately, Tippy's house made everyone's yards look poor in comparison. It was perfectly manicured with an extensive native plant collection. Plus, it was a pet project of Tippy's. Anything Tippy put her hand to was going to be done well.

Many of the garden club members were already in the backyard. But then, there was always a good turnout when Tippy was hostess. She put out spectacular spreads of food. And there was always an amazing speaker present. If it was sunny, she put out tents. If it was rainy, she gathered everyone inside her large, immaculate house.

Tippy greeted them as soon as they walked up. "*So* glad to see the two of you here. Miles, what a treat to have you here."

Miles gave her a polite smile. "What a treat to be here."

"No ill effects from last night?" Tippy asked in a low voice.

"We're all fine, I think," said Myrtle. "Although, it was a tremendous shock."

It hadn't actually been a tremendous shock. Myrtle had the unlikely habit of stumbling over bodies regularly. It was ghastly, and she felt sorry for Victoria. But not shocked. Still, it seemed like the kind of thing Tippy, who didn't come across bodies often, if at all, would expect to hear.

Tippy nodded solemnly. "I know what you mean. I didn't sleep a wink. How is Wanda holding up?"

"She was absolutely exhausted last night, but was all right this morning. I did invite her to come with me to garden club, but I think she wanted some alone-time."

"That's wise of her," said Tippy. She frowned as she looked at a serving table, which was laden with charcuterie boards. "I asked the staff to put out the desserts at the same time as the other food. Please excuse me while I chase them down."

Myrtle and Miles watched as Tippy, a bee in her bonnet, strode off toward her gracious home. "Someone's in trouble," said Miles mildly.

"Indeed. Apparently, it's hard to get good help these days. Of course, I suppose I'd know that, considering I'm saddled with Dusty and Puddin."

"I'm sure your yard will be in great shape by the time we return," said Miles. "Dusty appeared to be in full swing."

"Which is a good thing. Otherwise, I'd have felt like a fraud at garden club."

"It does sound like there will be a lot of gnomes gracing your front yard," said Miles.

"Everyone understands and excuses my yard art," said Myrtle with a sniff. "It has nothing to do with my gardening ability."

Tippy swiftly left the house again as a caterer scurried toward the serving table with a tray full of small desserts. An irritated pucker on her brow smoothed out as she briefly joined Myrtle and Miles again. "When we were leaving last night, I spoke with Ellie Thornhill and invited her to come today.

Maybe it would be good if you chatted with her? She might not know many people here."

Then, Tippy floated off to greet others.

Myrtle said, "I think it's a good idea if we chat with her regardless of how many people she knows here."

Miles lifted a brow. "And before she is in Erma's clutches?"

It looked as if Erma was heading in Ellie's direction.

"Miles, you must distract Erma."

Miles recoiled. "You could distract Erma."

"Then I won't be able to question Ellie, will I? Go on, you'll be fine. You've always been more immune to Erma than I am." She gave him a small shove, then hurried over to Ellie to pull her aside.

Chapter Ten

Ellie Thornhill was a petite woman in her forties. Her brown hair was streaked with silver and in a practical bob. She wore a ceramic pendant that might have been something she made. Myrtle vaguely remembered Ellie being an artist of some kind. And of course she was married to Mason, Victoria's contractor.

Myrtle gave her a smile. "Goodness, we're running into each other a lot, aren't we? I'm Myrtle Clover."

Ellie returned the smile. "Oh, I know who you are, Miss Myrtle. You're a legend in this town. And you're right—we're seeing quite a bit of each other, aren't we? Although I'd have preferred to skip the party we were at last night."

"Wasn't that horrid?" asked Myrtle in her best old lady voice. "Such a wretched thing to happen to poor Victoria during her lovely party. How on earth could something like that happen in dear Bradley?"

Ellie nodded gravely. "It's really shocking. I thought taking Tippy's invitation to garden club might be a pleasant distraction, but I have the feeling the only thing that can really take my mind off Victoria's death might be working in my studio."

"Oh, that's right. You're a potter, aren't you? What a marvelous thing, making art."

Ellie said, "It is. I can really get into a zone when I'm working with clay. I'm looking forward to doing that later today."

"How is Mason taking the news?"

Miles turned and gave Myrtle a look of abject suffering as his conversation with Erma festered. Myrtle gave him an encouraging smile before gazing back at Ellie.

"Mason?" Ellie's smile slipped a little. "Well, Victoria's death was startling to both of us, of course. We were stunned when we left Wisteria Hall. Such a terrible shock."

"The police seem to think Victoria's death was suspicious," said Myrtle, still in gossipy old lady mode. "Can you believe it? I had to admit to Red that I didn't notice anything before the lights went out. Then, after the power was gone, there was nothing *to* see. How about you? Were you able to fill in Red better than I could?"

Ellie was looking more uncomfortable now. "See anything?"

"Maybe somebody tampering with Victoria's beverages?" asked Myrtle sweetly.

Ellie gaped at her. "The police think Victoria was *poisoned*?"

"Well, *I* think that. I'm not sure what the police think. Often, they're several steps behind. I'm sure that's not their fault. They have all sorts of ridiculous protocol to follow. So . . . tampering? Any thoughts?"

Miles turned around again to give Myrtle an imploring look, but she waved him away.

"Goodness," said Ellie. "I had no idea. I was late to the buffet because I was discussing pottery with Adelaide."

"Adelaide is a potter?" asked Myrtle.

"No, just an admirer. I promised I'd run by her house with some pieces. I haven't had a public show lately, but I'll sometimes bring a small collection over for private shows. Anyway, I wasn't one of the first people at the buffet because we were chatting."

Myrtle said, "Were the two of you at the table during your conversation? Could you see Victoria's teacup or wine glass?"

"No, we were just standing in the back of the room. I didn't notice anything at all."

Myrtle sighed. It seemed as if most people she encountered were far less observant than she was. "How about Mason? You must have been paying attention to where your husband was."

Ellie flushed. "You can't think Mason had anything to do with this."

"Naturally. But if I knew where everyone was standing and sitting then it might be easier to piece it all together." Although now Myrtle was feeling as if Mason *was* more of a suspect. Ellie's reaction when Myrtle mentioned his name was rather telling.

Ellie considered this. "Mason was at the buffet talking with Benton, I think."

Myrtle said, "Got it. How about when everyone was seated at the table? Did you notice anything then?"

"That's when I was at the buffet with Adelaide."

Myrtle thought this was all most unhelpful. "Okay. So you've seen nothing at all."

Ellie's clouded features suddenly cleared. "Wait. You write for the paper, don't you?"

Myrtle preened a bit. She did like having her journalistic efforts recognized. "That's correct."

"This all makes more sense. You're trying to work on an article, aren't you?" Then Ellie frowned. "If I tell you things, you'll print them in the paper?"

"Gracious, no. Sloan wouldn't like that at all. It would be a bunch of hearsay, wouldn't it? Slanderous, perhaps. Sloan doesn't fancy any lawsuits. No, it just provides a bit of background to proceed with. And background can help a lot when you're trying to figure out a mysterious death."

Ellie said, "Investigative reporting must be tough."

"Oh, it is. But I do enjoy it." Myrtle paused. She felt as if they were going off-track. She tried to get back to the point. "What did you make of Victoria? Were you good friends?"

Ellie flushed again. "No, not at all. I mean, I didn't have anything against her, of course. But we didn't really run in the same circles."

"Were you surprised to get an invitation, then?"

"I was," Ellie said. "But I wasn't very surprised that Mason got one. He has business dealings with Victoria. I figured it was just a networking opportunity for her."

"Ah, that makes sense. Mason owns the construction company."

"That's right," said Ellie. "Thornhill Construction. I actually work for Mason's business, too. At least, I manage the finances. I don't have to wear a hard hat." She gave something of a humorless chuckle as if this was a joke she'd given many times before.

"That's nice of you to take time away from your art to help Mason out."

Ellie said, "Considering working there helps fund my art, it's a good tradeoff."

Myrtle glanced over at Miles, whose eyes were large in panic. A gaggle of old ladies had swarmed him now, flirting, bringing him small plates of food, and smiling up at him. At least Erma had wandered off to regale someone else about her digestive issues. Myrtle supposed Erma was jabbering about her tummy, although it could be any number of equally vile topics.

"Do you have any idea who might have wanted Victoria out of the way? How well do you know the other guests at the party?" asked Myrtle.

Ellie seemed relieved to have the topic shifted away from Mason and her. "I'm not especially close to anyone. But I do know them all just casually, you know. Bradley's such a small town."

"Right. Can you think of anyone there who might have wished Victoria ill?"

Ellie considered this. "I wouldn't want to say someone there was capable of murder," she said in a very low voice.

"Remember, this is all off-the-record. I'm simply looking for a bit of background."

Ellie nodded. "Well then, I'd say Walter Beaumont has good reason to want Victoria out of the way."

Myrtle said, "What makes you say that?"

"Victoria was setting out to destroy Walter's business. You know he owns The Bradley Inn. It's been the only place to stay in Bradley for ages. Victoria was pouring all this time and money into a spot that wouldn't just compete for guests. It would crush the competition."

Myrtle looked at Ellie thoughtfully. "I see. Victoria's Wisteria Hall would be far superior to The Bradley Inn in every way."

"Exactly. But it didn't just stop there. I hear a lot of gossip at the construction company. I understand Victoria was acquiring Walter's supplier contracts and that she'd hired away Walter's housekeeping staff, promising them higher wages."

"Mercy," said Myrtle. "What a blow that must have been to Walter. His family has owned that inn since I was a little girl. Actually, far before that. My mother was a young girl when his family built it." Myrtle paused. "But why would Victoria invite Walter to her party?"

"Why would she invite any of us? If you think about it, it was a strange assortment of people. Perhaps she was trying to make up for her bad behavior? Why did Victoria invite you?"

Myrtle said slowly, "I believe she invited me because I was vexed at not being invited."

"It's interesting, isn't it? Victoria didn't choose to invite her closest friends." Ellie shrugged. "But then, maybe it was just networking, like I said earlier."

"No one wants to network with me. Not unless they're looking for a grammar tutor or advice on buying garden gnomes."

Ellie said, "That's not entirely true, is it? We've just talked about the fact you work for the paper. Victoria might have wanted a member of the press there. And she didn't choose Sloan."

Myrtle straightened a bit. She did so much enjoy being called a member of the press. It almost made her forget what she was talking about. When she finally remembered, Tippy returned.

"Ellie, we can't have Myrtle hogging you all for herself. Let me introduce you to some ladies you might not know." And with that, Tippy directed Ellie away.

With a sigh, Myrtle turned to rescue Miles at long last. He was now beset upon by no fewer than five ladies, all competing for his attention.

"Miles!" she called out. "I need to talk with you about something most urgent."

Miles sprang into action, politely divesting himself of the ladies before practically sprinting in her direction.

"That took a while," he muttered.

"Ellie had plenty of things to say, although it took her a bit to warm up. I do think she's holding something back, though. Most likely about Mason."

"I think I'm about ready to leave garden club," said Miles darkly.

"We haven't even heard the program! Tippy would be aggravated if we left before the speaker. I'm sure she has someone wonderful lined up. She's the kind of person who lines up speakers months in advance."

Miles said, "Maybe we can say we've suddenly been taken ill."

"Then Tippy would think her lovely charcuterie boards are the culprit. That would make her positively lose her mind. No, the best course of action is to stay put. We can leave directly after the speaker." Myrtle pulled her phone out, peering at it. "I was right. Tippy found someone from the extension service to speak. It's on 'native plants for four-season interest.'"

"Fascinating," said Miles.

"You're a gardener yourself. I think you'll enjoy it far more than you think."

Miles, at least, paid attention to the talk. And once the speaker had finished, Myrtle was as good as her word. They left garden club, heading for Miles's car. He gave a sigh of relief. "I don't know when I was more ready to leave a place."

"You're just upset because you had a long Erma encounter."

Miles said, "You'd have felt the same if you'd had one."

"That's the thing, Miles. I *never* have a long Erma encounter. I always find a way to maneuver myself away as speedily as possible. It's the only way to survive meeting up with an Erma in the wild."

Miles said morosely, "The other ladies were just as bad."

"Now you're exaggerating. No one is as bad as Erma. Besides, they all fawn over you. I'd imagine that would be rather satisfying." Nobody fawned over Myrtle. Although she did like hearing compliments from former students from time to time.

"They were all gossiping about the party last night," said Miles, sounding glum. "And about the guests who attended."

"For heaven's sake! That's exactly what I want to know about. I had no idea you were engaged in such a productive conversation. Otherwise, I'd have joined in earlier."

Miles said, "It was a lot. One lady was saying Walter had to ask the bank for a business loan."

"Really? That's pretty high-quality gossip. I thought it would be more about who was having an affair with whom. That's more like what one hears about in Bradley."

"Oh, they discussed that, too. But the Walter thing went on and on. The Bradley Inn isn't going well, obviously, and Victoria offered to buy it from Walter for half of what it's worth. Apparently, Victoria saw herself as someone saving him from a bad situation."

Myrtle said, "I'm assuming Walter didn't see things that way."

"No. He was furious. He told Victoria that it was his family's legacy, and her offer was an embarrassment."

Myrtle said, "Gracious. Everyone's so hot tempered these days. So Walter was insulted and didn't consider the offer. Then Victoria poured a bunch of money into Wisteria Hall and was going to completely annihilate Walter's business."

"That's what I gathered. Ellie was saying Victoria was also hiring away Walter's staff and using his service providers. And I'm still annoyed Victoria stole Dusty away from me."

"At least you have him back again," said Miles.

Sure enough, when he pulled into Myrtle's driveway, the yard was neatly trimmed. Her entire collection of gnomes leered at them.

"Didn't he do a marvelous job?" said Myrtle. "He can really work when he's motivated. And all my darling gnomes are out, ready to remind Red that he's erred. Again."

Miles surveyed the crowded yard. "The ladies were talking about that, too."

"Well, they don't have anything else to do."

Miles continued. "They were speculating about what Red had done now. They were about to place bets on whether he'd threatened to send you to Greener Pastures again or if he'd planned on declaring your gnomes a public nuisance to have them hauled away by the city."

"Silly hens," grumbled Myrtle. "All right, enough of that. Let's plan our next step."

"My next step involves eating a meal and then taking a nap."

"Eating? I saw all those ladies plying you with food."

Miles said, "I wasn't actually eating any of it, though. I don't really eat food at gatherings. I'm always very conscious about getting something in my teeth or dropping my plate on the ground."

"Then last night must have been excruciating for you."

"At Wisteria Hall?" asked Miles. "Well, that was a bit different. Everyone was eating, and we were seated at a table. It's much more precarious when one is trying to balance a plate and a glass while talking to others."

"Mmm," said Myrtle absently. "The only thing is, I'm not such a big fan of your food and napping plan. I think we should strike while the iron is hot and speak with Walter Thornhill. We need to find out more about what he really thought about Victoria. It sounds like his business might be in desperate straits."

Miles balked. "I don't want to accost Walter at The Bradley Inn and pepper him with questions about a subject he likely doesn't want to talk about. Actually, I don't want to spend time with anyone at all. Between last night's party and the garden club meeting, it's been rather harrowing."

"More hyperbole! You're full of embellishments today, Miles. I tell you what. You'll go back and decompress for a while. Eat something, have some sweet tea. Then, after you're rejuvenated, we'll tackle Walter."

Miles didn't appear to like the idea of tackling Walter in any way. "It's still extremely nosy."

"Don't be silly! We're practically friends. We spent the evening with Walter yesterday, after all. I know—I'll represent the newspaper. I'll say I'm doing a series of stories on historic homes and businesses in Bradley. Walter will hop all over the idea of free advertising."

"That might work," said Miles grudgingly.

"It absolutely will. Why don't you pick me up at 3:30?"

Chapter Eleven

And so, hours later, Miles obediently drove Myrtle downtown to The Bradley Inn. It was a rambling two-story white clapboard building from the 1920s with a wide wraparound porch supported by square columns that needed some fresh paint.

The interior lobby had dark wood paneling and worn but genuine oriental rugs over hardwood floors that creaked underfoot. The area was full of mismatched antique furniture that appeared to be a mix of family pieces and estate sale finds. They worked harmoniously together, however.

"Wow, I haven't been in here for forever," said Myrtle, looking around.

"I'm surprised you've actually been in here at all," said Miles. "It's not as if you needed a place to stay when you're in Bradley."

"When I was a child, my father's mother would come visit and stay here. My parents' house wasn't big enough for hosting. So they'd bring me over for meals with my grandmother in the dining room here. I may have to steal a look at it before we go." She thought it over a second. "On second thought, maybe

I want to just keep the memory instead of discovering what it looks like now."

Miles was peering around. "I don't see Walter."

"It almost sounds as if you know Walter." This wasn't always the case. Miles tended to keep to himself, plus he hadn't always been a Bradley resident, so he had some catching up to do.

Miles said, "He's a member of the chess club. Although he doesn't have the best attendance record."

"I can't imagine Walter being very good with chess."

"He isn't," said Miles. "But it can be nice to play with someone who's poor at it. It's good for one's ego."

They walked farther into the dim interior of the inn. Finally, they saw a man in his 60s with calloused hands and kind eyes behind wire-rimmed glasses. He was in the lounge area, appearing to be dusting the dark wood end tables in there. Walter looked up quickly when they entered.

"Miss Myrtle! And Miles. What a pleasant surprise." He gave them a quizzical look. "You're clearly not here for a room, are you?"

Miles flushed at this and hurriedly shook his head. "No, no. We're just looking to talk with you."

Myrtle was amused by Miles's embarrassment. "That's right, Walter. Considering the way the party ended up, I didn't have the chance to speak with you. How have you been?"

The question apparently brought all of Walter's troubles to the forefront of his mind. There were deep grooves of worry around his eyes and on his forehead, as if his concerns had carved into his very features. "Oh, fine, I guess. Although the party was a shocker. And I still do miss Martha a lot."

Martha had been Walter's wife, and he'd lost her to cancer after nearly forty years of marriage. Myrtle nodded. "I know it must be a tough adjustment for you. The two of you were like peas in a pod."

Miles gave Myrtle a slightly reproving look. It didn't seem he'd known about Martha's demise and thought he should have been apprised of it. Myrtle carefully ignored him. People in Bradley were dropping like flies, and it wasn't Myrtle's job to fill Miles in. He should read the obituaries like she did.

Walter nodded sadly before quickly changing the subject. "Now, what can I do for you?"

Myrtle smiled. "It's more like what *I* can do for *you*. The *Bradley Bugle* is planning on running a series featuring our local business leaders. I thought we'd start with you."

Walter's face now creased in pleasure, perhaps by the thought of the feature, or perhaps because he was called a leader. "Why, that's wonderful, Miss Myrtle. I'd love to talk with you about the inn."

Myrtle had come prepared with her voice recording app at the ready. She could still jot down notes with the best of them; the problem was deciphering them afterwards. "Wonderful. Should we take a seat here, then?"

They relaxed into the old armchairs in the lounge. Myrtle turned on the app and directed Walter through a series of questions, which he happily answered in great detail. She'd have to trim the content later to keep the short feature from turning into an epic saga. Walter went on about the inn's history, some of its notable guests, and how his family had successfully helmed the business through various generations.

Finally, he wrapped up. "Will that work?"

"Most certainly," said Myrtle. "Naturally, I'll be editing for length. But it's all very interesting." Now she felt as if she were exaggerating nearly as much as Miles had been earlier.

Miles gave Walter an encouraging smile. "Will you be coming back to chess club?"

"Oh, we'll see. I'm not sure I'm up to being walloped at chess again," said Walter wryly. "I have to be in the right frame of mind for that. Maybe in the next couple of weeks. Also, that party really took it out of me. It might take a while for me to recover."

Myrtle gave him a sympathetic look. "Were you and Victoria very close?" She knew the exact opposite was likely true. Walter, after all, had seen Victoria as a problem. She was stealing his staff, his suppliers, and likely his business. On top of it all, she'd given him a lowball offer for his inn. She'd certainly not been in Walter's good graces.

Walter seemed startled by the notion that he could have been close to Victoria in any way. He hesitated so long that Myrtle added, "I mean, since she invited you to her party. I assume the two of you might have been friends."

He shook his head slowly. "No, I'm afraid we weren't really close. It would have been nice to have gotten to know her better. I knew her as someone who was part of the local business community, of course. She was a very driven woman." It didn't sound like much of a compliment coming from Walter. He frowned. "Miss Myrtle, have you gotten any updates from Red on how everything is going? What was Victoria's cause of death? She seemed as if she were in perfect health."

"I believe she *was* in perfect health, yes. From what I understand, Victoria was murdered at the party. Poisoned."

Miles shot Myrtle a look. Red had certainly said no such thing. But Myrtle was watching Walter for a reaction.

Walter gave one. His eyes bugged out behind his glasses, and he swallowed nervously. "Heavens. Was Red sure about that?"

"Positive. Has he been by to speak with you yet?"

Walter frowned. "By here? The inn? No. But of course I spoke with him after the party."

"Well, I'm sure he'll be back by to follow up. He'll be speaking with everyone who was at the party again, as a matter of protocol."

Walter's face nearly disappeared into the cavernous worry wrinkles now.

Myrtle said, "Sometimes, it's better to talk things out, you know. Be prepared for whatever is on its way. Would it be helpful to tell Miles and me your impressions of the party? That way, when you talk with Red or the state police, you'll feel a bit more confident." She was quite pleased with the way she'd phrased this. It was almost as if she were offering to give Walter practice instead of pressing him for information. She'd have to try this again.

Walter frowned. "The state police? I'd be a lot more comfortable talking to just Red."

"Oh, the SBI will likely be heading the interview. That's what we call the state police here." Myrtle loved feeling like an insider.

Walter said, "In that case, perhaps it would be helpful if I collected my thoughts prior to that. I'd hate to stumble over my words, and I'll be jittery enough talking with the SBI." He took a deep breath. "So, the party."

"You were surprised to get an invite," prompted Myrtle.

"Yes indeed," said Walter. "Victoria and I were just business acquaintances. I barely knew her, you see."

Miles nodded, but Myrtle frowned. "Really? I hate to bring this up, Walter, but you know how Bradley talks."

Walter looked alarmed and nodded.

"It seems people are saying that Victoria was interested in purchasing your inn. Perhaps she was wanting to eliminate the competition."

Walter swallowed again, looking miserable. "Well, that's true. Maybe wanted a spot in downtown and one on the lake." It sounded as if he was trying to give Victoria the benefit of the doubt.

Myrtle said sadly, "It seems people are also saying she gave you an insultingly low offer."

"I'm not sure if I'd say it was 'insulting.' I think I'd call it 'misguided.' But then, Victoria wasn't aware of all the local history wrapped up here. The importance of the inn to Bradley, you know. Since she was still something of an outsider, perhaps that's only natural. She probably didn't research what a good bid would be."

Miles cleared his throat. "Are you planning on selling the inn?"

"No, not at all. I was surprised when Victoria made the offer. I'll admit that it caught me off-guard, and perhaps I didn't respond as well as I should have. I was a bit upset."

Miles said, "That's understandable. The inn has been in your family for a long time."

Myrtle broke in impatiently. "Yes, it's very understandable. Still, you decided to attend the party. What made you do that?"

Walter sighed. "It was mostly curiosity. I'd heard Victoria had been working with Mason Thornhill to renovate her home to make it into a bed-and-breakfast. I wanted to see what it all looked like."

This would explain the alarmed expression on Walter's face from time-to-time during the tour Victoria had given them. Walter was perhaps seeing the writing on the wall, realizing she was going to end up getting the lion's share of the business when the bed-and-breakfast opened. Myrtle said, "Do you think Victoria invited you to show off her renovations? Maybe she wanted to make you see how nice her place was in the hopes you'd accept that low bid."

Walter shook his head. "I couldn't begin to speculate on what was going through Victoria's mind. Honestly, I was trying to be on my best behavior. I was embarrassed by the way I'd responded to Victoria's offer, and I wanted to show her that I could be pleasant and professional."

Myrtle said, "I'm sure the SBI will be asking where everyone was during the pivotal time."

"When was the pivotal time?"

Myrtle said, "That would have been when Victoria's teacup, or perhaps wine glass, were left on the table. Where someone could have easily tampered with it."

Walter frowned, looking as if he was searching his mind trying to find that bit of information. "Let's see. That's when the buffet was open in the conservatory. I suppose I was in line, talking to Benton Chambers. I've known him for quite a few years. Yes. We were talking and waiting our turn at the buffet."

"Did you notice anyone hovering around the table? Or tampering with Victoria's drinks?"

Walter looked regretful. "No. I wish I knew something. I was listening to Benton."

Myrtle thought that was extremely unfortunate. But then, Benton was the kind of person that made you listen when you were speaking with him. He had a lot of influence and lots of power. Naturally, Myrtle hadn't been affected by this. She didn't need a thing from Benton. But someone like Walter, whose business wasn't in great shape, might have hung on his every word.

Myrtle gave Miles a prompting look. She did like her sidekick to keep mum most of the time and not interfere. But occasionally, it was nice for him to help out. At this point, Myrtle felt they were striking out with information.

Miles said slowly, "Walter, what were your thoughts on Victoria? I'm trying to piece together exactly what I made of her. Unfortunately, that was both the first and last time that I'd met her."

Walter hesitated, as if trying to find just the right words. Perhaps he was still thinking about the state police and whether the SBI would pepper him with even tougher questions. That he should find some sort of answer for them. "I think I've tried to make sense of what I thought of Victoria, too. She was a very capable competitor, I'll say that. When she and I were together, I almost felt as if I were being outmaneuvered in a chess match."

He shook his head. "Victoria was very polished, very smart, very well-educated. She'd seen a lot of the world. In comparison, I have a very narrow view of the world. I've only worked for the family inn."

Miles gave him a sympathetic look, which was enough to make Walter continue on. "I think she was a very sharp business-woman. She hired away my housekeeper, Brenda." He sighed. "It's nearly impossible to replace Brenda. She'd been here for fifteen years and was truly excellent. Brenda told me Victoria offered her double wages."

"Mercy," said Myrtle. "That must have been hard to resist."

"Brenda was being upfront because she hoped I could counter-offer. She loved working at The Bradley Inn. But there was no way I could afford to give her that much of a raise. It hurt me that she left. I really valued her as an employee, but I was paying her top dollar for what I could afford. I didn't blame Brenda for leaving, though. She had to do what was best for her."

Myrtle said, "I suppose Brenda will be coming back to work here soon, then?"

Walter looked guilty at this. "Yes. Yes, she already called me this morning, having seen the news on social media. She asked for her old job back, and I leaped at the chance."

Myrtle said, "Have you heard of anyone who might have wanted to harm Victoria? Anyone who wished her ill?"

"This is all off the record, isn't it, Miss Myrtle?" Walter cast a nervous look at Myrtle's phone. The recording app was still running.

"Naturally. Sloan wouldn't let hearsay be printed in the paper."

"Of course not," said Walter hurriedly. He swallowed again. "I guess I'd have to say Benton Chambers. Although I'm sure he wasn't the one who poisoned Victoria. He'd never do such a thing. But he was probably relieved she was gone."

Myrtle raised her eyebrows. "What makes you say that?"

"Victoria, actually. It was when she visited the inn to give me the offer."

Miles asked, "When was that?"

"Oh, I guess it must have been a little over a week ago. Yes. Anyway, Victoria told me then that she had 'the planning commission in her pocket.' Her very words. Then she mentioned Benton specifically."

Myrtle said, "That seems like a very random thing for Victoria to bring up with you."

"I believe she was trying to make it clear that she could do what she wanted with the bed-and-breakfast. That she was in a better position than I was. It was shortly before she told me I should retire gracefully." There was bitterness in Walter's voice then.

"Gracious," said Myrtle. "It sounds like Victoria meant business."

"She was all about business," said Walter glumly. "But you know, my great-grandfather built this place with his own hands. It's my legacy. I can't imagine giving it up."

Miles asked politely, "Are your children planning on taking over the inn from you? In the future, I mean."

Myrtle gave him a quashing look. She felt that was quite enough from her sidekick. She'd rather hear more about what

Walter thought about Benton and Victoria's business connection.

Walter said, "No, my kids don't want it. Martha and I were always so sorry that they moved away as soon as they left for college. They had no interest in Bradley. One's in Atlanta and the other in Charlotte. They headed for big cities and rarely come back to visit. They don't want the business."

"So, eventually, you *will* be selling?" asked Miles.

"Yes, but on my own terms," said Walter, sounding stubborn. "Or maybe I won't. Maybe I'll just work here until I drop dead. Then selling the inn will be my kids' problem. I don't think I have it in me to sell it. It makes me sad just thinking about it. My father was always so proud of the inn. I felt honored when he passed the reins over to me."

Walter looked at his watch. "Well, I should get going. I need to make some phone calls. It was good talking to the two of you. I feel a lot more prepared now for any interviews with the police."

Myrtle said, "It was our pleasure, Walter. And be looking out for that feature in the paper soon."

Chapter Twelve

Minutes later, Myrtle and Miles were back in the car. Myrtle said, "Well, that was interesting."

"I feel rather sorry for Walter," said Miles as he steered his sedan toward Myrtle's house.

Myrtle said, "Yes, he did act kind of pitiful. But there's something about Walter that annoys me. He takes everything lying down. The way he's floating around that old inn like a ghost instead of fighting for it."

"What could he do? Everything seems out of his hands."

Myrtle said, "For starters, there's always advertising."

"It didn't sound like he was rife with money."

Myrtle said, "All right then, social media. Social media doesn't cost a thing and can generate plenty of views. He can't simply expect that The Bradley Inn is going to get all the hotel business in town."

"It's the only hotel *in* town," observed Miles helpfully.

"Yes, yes, I know that. But it's not the only place to *stay* in town. People rent out their houses and whatnot. Walter appears to live in the past. It's all very passive."

Miles said, "It sounds like he's mourning Martha. Which I hadn't even realized." He gave Myrtle a side-eye.

"For heaven's sake, Miles. I knew you were going to get hung up on that. I've told you before that you should be reading the obituaries. It's always the first thing I read in the newspaper every morning."

"What a cheerful way to start your day."

Myrtle said, "Actually, it is. It serves as a wonderful reminder that none of us are guaranteed time on this planet. We need to seize the day. What do you do when you get up in the morning?"

"Seize my coffee. Then perhaps the sudoku."

Myrtle said, "Well, start it out with the obits. I have the feeling it will change your priorities."

They were now pulling up at Myrtle's house. "Home sweet home," she said. "And my darling gnomes make me smile."

Miles said, "I hesitate to ask what our next steps are. You're not planning anything else today, are you?"

"No, we've done quite enough. But I do think we should speak with Mason Thornhill tomorrow morning, bright and early."

Miles sighed. "I was afraid you'd say that. I don't even know the man."

"As a reminder, he owns Thornhill Construction. He's the one who renovated Victoria's home to make it a bed-and-breakfast. Or rather, his team did. I'm sure Mason must have been the one supervising."

Miles balked. "I don't want to show up at a construction site to push Mason for information."

"I would think Mason is too far up the food chain for him to spend much time at construction sites. No, we'll beard the lion in his den. At his office."

"Fun times," said Miles with a sigh.

Myrtle said her goodbyes and walked inside, admiring her gnomes as she went. Her favorites alternated, but the one she most enjoyed for the time being was a scholarly-looking gnome with tiny spectacles and a book. She'd nicknamed him Professor Whiskers.

She looked around inside. The house was at least respectable-looking, although far from the standard at which she'd like to keep it. That Puddin never really got things sparkling.

Myrtle made a quick phone call to Sloan, informing him of the feature she was planning on The Bradley Inn and Walter.

Sloan said, "Is he going to advertise with us, Miz Myrtle? Usually, we're looking for a quid pro quo for that kind of thing."

"This is how it works: we'll feature Walter. Business will increase. Walter will be amazed at how lucrative being featured in the newspaper is. He'll then purchase advertising. Just like that."

"Just like that," said Sloan, sounding weary.

Myrtle said, "Now, make sure to run my article on Victoria's death on the front page tomorrow."

"No worries, that's a big story. But there will be Red fallout."

Myrtle said, "Don't be concerned about Red. I know how to handle him."

But Sloan didn't sound at all sure.

The next morning, Myrtle had finished her coffee when she called Lieutenant Perkins. He was usually more forthcoming than Red with providing information on cases. She imagined forensics had determined Victoria's cause of death by this point, surely.

Perkins answered immediately. "Mrs. Clover. How are you this morning?"

"Oh, fairly good. But how are you doing? Have you been able to get any sleep since that wretched party at Victoria's? What a dreadful night and storm that was. And you had to go traipsing around in it." Myrtle clucked at this.

"Just part of the job, I'm afraid. Of course, Red had to be out in it quite a bit, too."

"Yes, I suppose so." Myrtle was still too annoyed with Red to feel sorry he'd gotten rained on. "How's the investigation going? Is the workload too bad? I'm sure you're swamped with the Victoria situation?"

Perkins politely answered, "It's manageable. We have a good team over here working on it. And progress is being made."

"On that note, I was wondering if a cause of death has been determined for poor Victoria. Red did mention that you were all treating it as a suspicious death. I, of course, am convinced it must have been poison."

Perkins said, "Yes, forensics did confirm poisoning. There were nightshade derivatives in her teacup. Victoria's death occurred roughly thirty minutes after ingestion. But please keep that all under your hat, if you would."

Myrtle clucked again. "Mercy. How awful. But not surprising. Do you have any leads? I know it's early, so don't worry if the team hasn't gotten that far."

"Unfortunately, I can't discuss active investigation details. But we're working on it." Perkins paused. "Could you help steer me in any particular direction, Mrs. Clover? You've always had a gift for this."

Myrtle preened. "Why, thank you. But I'm sure you're on the right track. The suspect was at that party, and I doubt it was a member of the staff." She stopped for a moment, thinking. "Gracious. Did you have to interview all the staff at the party?"

"I'm afraid so. But none of them seemed to have a connection to Victoria except through the catering company." Then Perkins said, "Sorry, Mrs. Clover, duty calls. I have another call coming in."

"Certainly. Take care, Perkins."

"And you, Mrs. Clover. Don't take any risks."

After getting off the phone with Perkins, Myrtle called Miles. "Let's go for a drive."

Miles groaned. "Why don't I like the sound of that?"

"I've no idea. It's a minor thing, after all. A lovely drive on a lovely day. I'd like to see what Victoria's mansion looks like in the daylight."

Miles said, "Surely, you've seen it in the daylight before. The house predates you by at least a few years."

Myrtle scowled at this. "You're trying to get under my skin. You know it dates back to the 1800s. But you won't annoy me this morning. I'm in an excellent mood. Perkins just told me that Victoria was indeed poisoned."

"Confirmed poisoning makes you happy?"

Myrtle said, "Being proven correct makes me happy. Let's go for a drive."

Miles demurred. "Won't the police still be there? They won't want us at Wisteria Hall."

"I'm not talking about trekking through the grounds. Merely a drive-by. And then, perhaps, a trip to the grocery store."

Miles said, "I'm starting to discern your true reason for wanting to go out. You're out of food, aren't you? You could just ask. I'm happy to take you there."

"I did have a very meager breakfast of grits."

Miles said, "Isn't grits a normal breakfast for you?"

"Grits made with *milk* is a normal breakfast. Grits made with water is something else. And I couldn't even put butter or cheese in it because I was out of both. It was most aggravating."

"I'll be right there."

Minutes later, Myrtle was walking out to Miles's car with a purposeful stride, her cane tapping on the front walk, when Scotty the rooster erupted at her from behind one of her larger gnomes. It gave a loud, outraged crow, flapping its wings at her.

Miles quickly got out of his car, looking alarmed. "Here, let me help you, Myrtle."

"No need. I can handle a rooster. Besides, you're making him more agitated."

This was true. Scotty had whirled around and given Miles an evil stare. Miles obediently climbed back into the car, watching the interaction warily.

Scotty blocked Myrtle's path, his chest puffed up, taking a territorial stance.

Myrtle summoned up her teaching voice. Giving the rooster a steely glare, she said, "Stop at once, Scotty. Bad!"

Scotty, perhaps recognizing alpha energy from Myrtle, backed down with dignity.

"Scotty! Not again!" called Elaine from across the street. She hurried over and gathered him into her arms. "So sorry, Myrtle."

"No problem, Elaine. Good luck with your livestock."

Elaine sighed. "Yes. It does seem to be going poorly right now. I'll need to reinforce my chicken coup." She headed back to the house as the rooster started pecking at her arms.

"You all right?" asked Miles as Myrtle got into the car.

"Certainly. I must say there's a part of me that respects Scotty a bit. At least one creature in this neighborhood respects authority."

"I'm just glad you could escape unscathed." Miles pulled out of the driveway, heading toward downtown.

"Where on earth are you going?"

"The store. You don't have any food. It seems to be the priority right now," said Miles.

"I'd rather view Wisteria Hall now. Then we can go to the Piggly Wiggly and get provisions."

So Miles drove them over to the mansion. It was indeed a beautiful day. The morning air was crisp and pleasant. A few early-fall leaves were turning. When they reached the mansion, Miles came to a stop outside the driveway.

"I do still see lots of crime scene tape," he said apprehensively.

"Which is why this is as close as we'll get. It really is a lovely house, isn't it? As you mentioned so gallantly, it's been here my whole life, of course. But it wasn't always in such good shape.

Victoria really did do an excellent job getting it renovated." She stopped, peering down the long driveway to the base. "I believe someone is down there."

Miles said, "Well, that's none of our business. It's probably some sort of investigator."

"No, I believe it's Mason Thornhill. Look, that's his van."

"Then he's here working," said Miles. "We should let him get on with his job."

But Myrtle wasn't so sure. "Why on earth would he be here? Victoria can't pay him for further work, obviously."

"I don't particularly want to find out. We look nosy enough, as is."

Myrtle peered through the windshield. "Look. He's getting in the van and backing up."

Miles gave a beleaguered sigh.

As Mason reached the top of the driveway, Myrtle rolled down her window. "Mason! Yoo-hoo!"

Chapter Thirteen

Mason gave a slight grimace before reluctantly rolling down his own window. He was a ruggedly handsome man in his mid-forties with the kind of lean, muscular build that came from physical work instead of gym memberships. "Miss Myrtle. What are you doing here?"

"Hello, Mason. You remember Miles from the party."

The two men gave small nods of acknowledgment.

Myrtle continued, "I wanted to see Wisteria Hall in the daylight. Your construction team did an absolutely marvelous job with the renovation. It's never looked better. And I've been around for a long time."

Mason gave her a smile. "Well, thank you, Miss Myrtle. That's high praise coming from you. We did put in a lot of hard work. I just can't believe what happened. Now I'm wondering about the house's future."

"Yes, it's simply tragic, isn't it? Poor, poor Victoria."

Miles shot Myrtle a look as if she were being a bit over-the-top. Myrtle changed gears. "I was wondering what you might have to still do over here? Surely, you're not still working on Wisteria Hall. Not under the circumstances."

"I'm not doing any further work, no. But I needed to retrieve some tools and materials we left behind. Since the news of Victoria's death is out, I was worried someone might come by and steal them." He glanced back at the house, an unreadable look on his face. "After what happened at the party, this is the last place I wanted to be, believe me."

Miles said, "I'd imagine not."

"You must be especially stunned, Mason," said Myrtle. "Having worked closely with Victoria for such a long time."

Mason frowned. "Our business relationship was a good one, yes."

"Someone else has suggested that Victoria's party guests were people who she was interested in networking with." Myrtle gave a tittering laugh. "Apart from Miles and me, of course. Unless she wanted grammar help or information on architecture."

"Engineering," said Miles tightly.

Mason said, "I wasn't sure exactly how Victoria came up with her guest list. It seemed kind of random to me." He shook his head. "I can't believe she's gone. I guess it must have been a heart attack? The police didn't provide any information when they were talking to me."

"I'm afraid her death wasn't from natural causes at all," said Myrtle. "It was murder." Perkins didn't tell her she couldn't share that it was a homicide, only that she should keep quiet about poison.

Mason looked rather stunned at this. "You can't be serious. Who would want to kill Victoria? And why would someone do something like that at a party with everyone there?"

"Desperation?" asked Myrtle. "Plus, I've gotten the impression Victoria could be challenging to deal with. Did you find her so, Mason?"

Mason flushed. "Not challenging. I'd say Victoria was somebody who knew exactly what she wanted. And she wasn't afraid of saying what that was. She wanted the job done right and didn't care how long it took to get it finished."

"She sounds like a perfectionist," said Miles.

"She was."

Myrtle tilted her head to one side. "I do find perfectionists difficult to deal with, though, don't you? Nothing is ever right for them."

Mason shrugged. "It wasn't too bad. Other clients have been far worse. She'd change her mind about fixtures and finishes, often when the work was nearly complete. But that's not unusual in my business. Sometimes the client will see the fixture in place and decide it doesn't work. Victoria wanted crown molding added to every room, not just the main areas, and that was fairly late in the process. And she was a stickler for period-correct details. But Thornhill Construction can handle that kind of challenge."

Myrtle asked, "Was Victoria the sort of person to make a good deal of after-hours calls?"

Mason flushed again. "What do you mean? Victoria and I didn't know each other outside work."

Myrtle raised an eyebrow. "Didn't she want immediate responses to non-urgent issues?"

"Oh, I see. No, nothing like that. Like I said, Victoria wasn't in a huge hurry to finish the project. She just wanted it done right."

Myrtle said, "Did you see anything unusual at the party? Anybody behaving strangely?"

Mason shook his head. "Nothing like that. In fact, I was having a good time. I was looking forward to the séance thing. And I had a good conversation with Benton Chambers."

"So more business, then."

"That's right. Benton is a busy guy. When you get the unexpected chance to talk to him without interruptions, you take it. He and I chatted together when we were waiting for food, then afterwards at the table. I was pretty focused on that, since I want to get some permits pushed through. I didn't notice anything unusual." Then he frowned. "Well, there was Walter. You know, the guy who owns the inn. He didn't seem to be in a party mood."

Myrtle said, "I'm not sure Walter has had much to feel festive over lately. After all, Victoria's bed-and-breakfast might have put him out of business."

"True," said Mason. "But the guy just looked miserable. He kept trying to talk to Victoria, but it looked like she was avoiding him." He glanced at his wristwatch. "Well, it was nice talking to y'all, but it's time for me to run. I've got other sites I need to check on. See you later."

With a quick wave, Mason drove away. Miles turned and headed back toward downtown and the grocery store.

"Well, that was very helpful," said Myrtle.

"Was it? It didn't seem like much to me. We already knew Walter has been worried about his business. He was probably wanting to ask Victoria to let him have his housekeeper back. Naturally she wouldn't want to talk with him about that. Although it's peculiar to me that she invited him at all."

Myrtle said, "I have the feeling it was in Victoria's nature to rile people up. Maybe she wanted to show off her newly-renovated home to Walter and rub it in his face. But I wasn't actually talking about what Mason said about Walter. I was talking about something else."

Miles frowned. "*Was* there anything else? It sounds like he was focused on Benton at the party, not on Victoria's teacup. He mentioned Victoria was a perfectionist, but that's hardly a surprise. She fit the part."

"No, no. I'm talking about the fact Victoria and Mason were having an affair."

Miles blinked. "I listened carefully throughout the entire conversation. I'm certain Mason made no mention of having an affair with Victoria or anyone else."

"Of course he didn't. What nonsense, Miles. But didn't you note how he flushed when I asked if Victoria called him after-hours? It was quite obvious."

Miles said, "I think you've been watching too many soap operas."

"I tell you, I saw it. Which certainly means Mason makes an excellent suspect. Maybe Victoria was threatening to tell Ellie about the affair. Or maybe Victoria was simply being indiscreet. Mason might have wanted to shut her up. It's one thing to have an affair with somebody, but something entirely different to lose one's marriage over it. It seems to me that Mason and Ellie have a good life together."

Miles said, "Then it's odd Mason would go astray."

"That's what happens sometimes, though. Anyway, it's all very interesting. Now we just need to find out for sure."

"How on earth do you plan to do that?" asked Miles, looking queasy. "You're not going to ask Mason about it, are you?"

"I'd never be so indiscreet and you know it. I'll just see if I can find out through the grapevine."

The Piggly Wiggly was a zoo. Myrtle steered through the obstacle course of grocery carts with Miles trailing behind her. She had a lot to buy and a teacher's pension to stretch. Every purchase required scrutiny. She bought what was on sale or what offered the best value per ounce.

Miles became fidgety.

"We'll be out of here before long, Miles. Why don't you just wait for me in the car?"

"I thought I'd give you a hand with the bags," said Miles.

"You can do that when you spot me walking out the door with them. If I try to speed up the process, I'm going to forget all the things on my mental grocery list."

Myrtle breathed a sigh of relief as Miles finally caved and headed for the exit. But the next minute, her shopping was forgotten altogether when she spotted Benton Chambers browsing the cocktail mixers section like a man with a problem to drown.

"Just the person I wanted to see," said Myrtle in a peppy voice.

Chapter Fourteen

Benton had apparently been deep in thought because he jumped violently. "Miss Myrtle," he said. "Didn't see you." He looked as if he'd preferred to keep it that way.

Benton was never one of Myrtle's favorite people. He always appeared to lump her in under the 'Tippy's silly friends' category, which was decidedly where she didn't belong. He likely would have hidden somewhere in the Piggly Wiggly if he'd seen her coming. But this time, he'd be right to want to avoid her. She had some hard questions for Benton.

"It's good to see you, Benton. Planning a party?"

"Pardon?"

"A party," said Myrtle louder. Perhaps Benton was losing his hearing. "Because of all the mixers you're buying."

Benton gave a short laugh. "Tippy and I have cocktails at home."

"I see." Although, really, Myrtle didn't. She would occasionally consume a small sherry in one of her mother's tiny, ancient crystal glasses. But that was the extent of alcohol for Myrtle. She moved on. "I wanted to talk with you about Victoria's ill-fated party." Usually, she wanted to be more subtle in her approach.

But she had the feeling that Benton was going to spring away on some pretense at the soonest opportunity.

"Ah," he said, as if he'd imagined she'd want to gossip about it. He sighed, looking longingly toward the checkout lane.

"Yes. I didn't realize you and Tippy were so close to Victoria. At least, I presume you were close, since you had an invitation."

Benton raised an eyebrow. "I didn't realize you and Miles were so close to her."

He was really being most irritating today. "We weren't."

Benton shrugged. "So Victoria wasn't inviting close friends. She had her own reasons for the motley assortment."

"I suppose so." Myrtle very much wanted to know what those were. Victoria seemed to be networking or showing off. Perhaps both. She continued. "If you weren't close to her, what was your connection?"

"Oh, Tippy was connected with Victoria. No surprise there. Tippy is connected with everyone in Bradley." Benton said this in a matter-of-fact tone, but there was a tinge of something admiring there. Myrtle supposed Tippy's networking had been very beneficial to Benton in all his political roles in town.

"And you?"

"Me?" he asked.

Myrtle said, "I'm sure you were probably connected with Victoria, too. In a business regard."

Now, Benton was looking at her through narrowed eyes. "Only distantly. Victoria was converting Wisteria Hall to a bed-and-breakfast. There were permits and zoning issues involved, and you're probably aware, I lead the zoning commission. But aside from the business relationship, I barely knew Victoria."

"What was your impression of her?"

Benton's eyes narrowed further, so they were practically lost in his puffy features. "You're not writing a story for the newspaper, are you Myrtle? These are fairly pointed questions."

"It's all about background, that's all. Naturally, Victoria's death is something the paper wants to cover. But Sloan always wants to do that very professionally."

Benton gave an involuntary snort. But then, Myrtle was sure she'd heard Benton's voice in the background on some occasions when she'd called Sloan and he'd been frequenting the bar near the newspaper office. Clearly, he didn't think of Sloan as much of a professional. But he appeared to offer details, for whatever reason.

"Victoria? Hard as nails. Didn't like hearing no."

Myrtle said, "I'm guessing you tried not to tell her no, then. Considering she was a very influential person in town."

Benton said, "*I'm* a very influential person in town. But to answer your question, I tried to smooth things over with the permits and the zoning requests. That wasn't because of Victoria, but because Bradley needs more hospitality options. The way Victoria presented the plan for Wisteria Hall, it would function not only as a spot for Bradley tourists to stay, but also as a venue for weddings and other events. As you know, Bradley doesn't have many event spaces."

Myrtle guessed Bo's Diner wouldn't count as an event space. Unless one was planning a family reunion or some such. "You heard Victoria's death is murder."

"Naturally. I hear things, as you'd imagine, in my position. Plus, I didn't think for a second that a woman of Victoria's age and condition would drop dead. Murder made the most sense."

Myrtle said, "What might you have noticed at the party? Did you see anyone acting suspiciously?"

Benton sighed. "Myrtle, I was just trying to make it through the party. I hadn't really wanted to attend in the first place. I spoke with Mason about various permits during the lead-up to dinner. It felt like I was in my office doing work, except I was stuck there and couldn't leave."

"It wasn't as if we were locked in."

Benton gave a short laugh. "I might as well have been. Tippy would never be rude enough to leave a party early. I could have feigned illness, I suppose. But then the storm started up, the lights went out, and Victoria was dead."

Myrtle thought for a second. "Tippy, of course, is on the town council. Did Victoria need both your and Tippy's support for the bed-and-breakfast?"

He gave her a grudging look of respect. "That's correct. Tippy was going to be the swing vote on the council for the zoning change."

"I'm surprised to hear the council wasn't wanting to wholeheartedly support the bed-and-breakfast."

Benton said, "Well, some of folks really felt badly for Walter and The Bradley Inn. Walter's family has been an important part of this town for ages. They didn't want him to lose business because of a fancy new place."

"Wisteria Hall is hardly new. It's older than The Bradley Inn."

Benton gave her an impatient look. "Yes, but it's updated. The Bradley Inn wouldn't have been able to compete. Plus, Victoria is a relative newcomer to Bradley still. Walter's family has been here for generations. Tippy was going to be the swing vote, like I said."

"Who do you think might have wanted Victoria out of the way? Walter?"

Benton winced. "I really don't think Walter Beaumont is a killer. I don't think *any* of those folks we attended the party with are murderers, in fact. I told Red he should be looking at the staff. Maybe one of them stole something from Victoria. She might have found out about it and was planning on turning in the culprit. Surely that would be a motive."

"I think that's rather unlikely, don't you? The catering staff were all just hired for the party—they weren't long-term staff. And Victoria's housekeeper was Brenda, who'd been working for Walter for ages."

Benton gave a sigh. "Okay. I still don't think any of the guests would have killed anybody. But I will say Adelaide had reason to be annoyed by Victoria. And she was. Annoyed, I mean."

"Because of Victoria's plans to convert the house into a bed-and-breakfast?"

"Correct. Adelaide always fights change of any kind. It appears to be in her personal makeup. She had a hissy fit when we put in that new traffic light on Sycamore and Elm. She fought the library expansion. She dislikes property improvements. Adelaide has been at every single town council meeting that I can remember," said Benton.

"That sounds very involved of her."

"It's very *annoying* of her," corrected Benton.

"So you're saying Adelaide was publicly opposed to Wisteria Hall becoming a bed-and-breakfast."

Benton said, "She certainly was. But it was personal to her, too. After all, Wisteria Hall had been in her family for generations before it was sold. It was her family legacy. She didn't want it commercialized. She didn't want it renovated. She wanted it left totally as-is."

"But it wasn't hers anymore."

"Try telling Adelaide that. There's also the fact that she lives next door. She didn't want traffic resulting from having people driving there. She didn't want staff coming and going. The whole idea made her apoplectic. She was getting all her neighbors stirred up against it, too. Adelaide kept telling them Victoria's changes were historically inappropriate," said Benton. He gave another longing look at the checkout line. "Look, I need to grab the rest of the things on my list and go. Hope you have a good day, Miss Myrtle." With that, he was gone.

Myrtle kept thinking about their encounter, however. This made her progress through the grocery aisles long and painstaking. Her brain was having a tough time pivoting between what she needed on the breakfast food aisle and what she'd gleaned, however painstakingly, from Benton.

When she finally meandered out of the store, she wasn't entirely sure what she'd picked up. She hoped she had enough to create at least a meal or two. It seemed that whenever she strayed off a mental list, she ended up with a bunch of odds and ends that were no good on their own.

Miles leaped out of his car to put the bags in his trunk. "That took a lot longer than I expected," he said. "I was about to come check on you."

"Hmm? Oh. That's because I came across Benton Chambers."

Miles now looked relieved that he'd sat in the car to wait. "You questioned him?"

"Naturally. That's the whole point." She got into the passenger side, still mulling over her conversation with Benton.

A minute later, Miles got into the vehicle, and they started for Myrtle's house. "Did you find out anything important?" he asked, glancing her way.

"It was like pulling teeth. But I did get some nuggets, yes. I discovered Victoria needed both Tippy and Benton's support to get the bed-and-breakfast approved."

"Really?" asked Miles, frowning. "Benton I can understand. But Tippy? She's just one person on the council."

"And the swing vote. No wonder Victoria had them at her party. She probably designed the whole evening around them. Benton and Tippy were key to getting her plans off the ground."

"Got it," said Miles. He pulled into Myrtle's driveway, looking warily around for wayward roosters. Not seeing any, he asked, "Anything else?"

"Benton thought Adelaide really had it in for Victoria."

"Enough to murder her?" Miles sounded shocked.

"Old ladies can be dangerous," said Myrtle. "You should know that. Besides, Victoria was poisoned. It wasn't as if she were overpowered in some way. Adelaide most certainly could have done it. Benton, however, stopped short at saying Adelaide was a murderer."

"Why did he think she was upset with Victoria?"

Myrtle said, "Several reasons. Adelaide is change-adverse, has fond memories of Wisteria Hall, and didn't want the traffic inherent in having a commercial entity next door."

"Very succinctly put."

"I was an English teacher," said Myrtle with a sniff. Then she sighed. "Somehow, I feel like a rest, though. Today has been a lot."

"Well, you spoke to both Mason and Benton. That *was* a lot."

Myrtle said, "I don't think Mason was the problem. But that Benton does have the ability to get on my last nerve. I'm not sure how Tippy has handled him for so many years."

"Tippy is a very efficient person. And handles everyone extremely well. It's her gift."

Myrtle said, "One of many."

"Plus, I don't think Tippy spends all that much time with Benton."

"True," said Myrtle thoughtfully. "The key is staying as far from Benton as humanly possible." She peered at Erma's house, stiffening. "Curtain flutter. Run."

"We can't. We have groceries to unpack."

"I cannot endure an Erma encounter today," said Myrtle, hopping out of the car. "Pop the trunk, Miles. Grab and dash."

Too late. Erma was hurrying outside, trilling delightedly. "Myrtle and Miles! Just the people I wanted to see."

"Can't stop, Erma. Groceries," said Myrtle.

"I can help with groceries!"

Unacceptable. It meant Erma would be inside Myrtle's house. Myrtle couldn't countenance that, not right now. "Miles and I have it, don't we, Miles?"

"We do," agreed Miles firmly.

"Nonsense! I'm younger than both of you."

Debatable, especially where Miles was concerned. Myrtle was preparing to throw herself bodily in front of the trunk when a belligerent squawk erupted from behind a gnome.

"Scotty!" sang out Myrtle.

Erma's face was a mask of alarm. "That chicken?"

"Rooster," said Myrtle in a satisfied tone. "I'm afraid he has a temper."

Scotty launched himself at Erma, wings flapping, beak jabbing at her ankles. She shrieked and ran.

Then Pasha spotted her nemesis. The cat tore after the rooster, still chasing Erma. Erma was now wailing about her allergies.

Elaine burst out of the house, sandwich still in hand. "Scotty!" she cried out.

"Miles, let's grab the groceries," said Myrtle.

Soon, laden with bags, the two of them rushed into the house. Myrtle slammed the door behind them, locking it as soon as she did. "That was a narrow escape," she muttered. "Remind me we simply can't sit in the car. Bad things happen when we linger outside."

They put away the groceries, both of them quietly trying to catch their breath from the rush to get everything inside. Eventually, the rooster's crowing and Erma and Elaine's voices died down.

"The crisis seems to be resolved," said Miles, looking relieved. "I was worried I'd be needed to capture the rooster."

"You're not derelict in duty. You were helping an old lady get her groceries indoors. And it's most appreciated. Now, as a reward, we should watch *Tomorrow's Promise*. We owe it to ourselves."

Miles looked relieved. "So you really meant it? You're done for the day?"

"I am. We'll watch our show. Tomorrow, though, we should start fresh and early."

Miles seemed sorry to hear this. "If we start too early, people won't be up and about."

"Adelaide will be. She's another old person who doesn't sleep. She and I have discussed it before. We should start with her."

Miles said, "But you spoke with her at the party. She didn't seem to have noticed much that would help."

"That's before I knew she had such a problem with Victoria's bed-and-breakfast. Now I can ask her more targeted questions. I also want to find out when Victoria's memorial service will be. Surely that must be coming up."

"Is someone giving a memorial service?" asked Miles with a frown. "Victoria didn't have any family in town, did she? And she wasn't married. Did she even have friends? They weren't at the party, if she did."

"I'm guessing Victoria was the kind of person who had allies, not friends. I do remember hearing Victoria had an older brother. We should check online and see if her obituary and service information is posted." Myrtle proceeded to do that on her phone.

Miles said, "Maybe there won't be a service."

"Of course there'll be a service. This is the South. There's always a service."

Miles said, "Victoria didn't seem to be the type to attend church."

"It doesn't matter. She was the type to make *donations* to a church. The type of person who wanted influence in every aspect of town. I guarantee you there'll be a service. She'd surely haunt that brother of hers if he didn't set one up." She frowned at her phone. "Sure enough. The service is tomorrow."

"Do they even have Victoria's body back from forensics?" asked Miles.

"It's to be a memorial service. Body-free. And a reception following the service in the church hall."

"So it *is* at a church?" Miles asked in surprise.

"Like I said, it's the South, Miles."

"I've always lived in the South," said Miles.

"Atlanta doesn't count."

They made plans for Miles to take Myrtle to the service the following day. Then they settled down to watch the next fascinating installment of *Tomorrow's Promise*.

Chapter Fifteen

The next morning, Myrtle studied her closet with a frown. The problem with wearing one's funeral outfit to a party was that, when the hostess of said party was inevitably murdered, there was no clean outfit to wear. She had neglected to think of this the day before, so her pantsuit was still in the hamper.

Her other options didn't seem eligible for consideration. In fact, they were rather loud, especially for a memorial service. She had a pair of navy slacks, which would work fine. Since it wasn't a graveside, she didn't have to consider the weather as a factor, meaning she could wear her green jacket with the navy pants. That's not ordinarily a color combination Myrtle would tolerate, but these were desperate times. Then she realized she couldn't find a navy shell to wear under the jacket.

"For heaven's sake," she muttered.

It simply wouldn't do. She was short on time, but thought she might wash and dry the outfit she'd worn to the party. However, when she pulled them out, she realized she'd torn a seam on the shoulder of the top at some point that evening.

Myrtle muttered again. There was nothing for it but to buy something else. But because she'd spent so much at the grocery store and had a couple of weeks to go before she received her retirement check, she was going to have to shop at the thrift store. She had no problem with this, other than the fact that she needed to wash and dry whatever she bought there.

She called Elaine. On the other end, she heard Jack singing along to a TV show and smiled.

"Myrtle!" said Elaine. "I'm glad you called. I've been wanting to talk to you. Life and a particular rooster seem to get in the way every time I pick up the phone."

"I can only imagine. Listen, Elaine, could you do me a tremendous favor? I need a ride to the thrift store for a new outfit for Victoria's memorial service. Are you available?"

Elaine could apparently hear the stress in Myrtle's voice. Myrtle did dislike being late. "I'll be right there."

Elaine was as good as her word. She had Jack in tow, but it was always a tremendous pleasure for Myrtle to spend time with her grandson. As Elaine drove, Myrtle chatted animatedly with Jack for a couple of minutes about trucks and dinosaurs. And dinosaurs driving trucks. And what it would be like if there were both flying trucks and flying dinosaurs.

Elaine pulled into the parking lot outside the store. "Do you need advice on what to buy? Or is this the kind of thing where you need to run in and grab something?"

"I'm afraid it's the second category. But thanks. I should be right out."

That apparently wasn't to be, though. First, the thrift store was in a state of complete disorganization. That wasn't usually the case. Myrtle frowned, her gaze raking over the aisles. She had a foggy recollection of the store's changing ownership. Obviously, the new owner was exceedingly lax.

Another issue was that Puddin was in the shop. And Puddin was apparently in the mood to chat.

As Myrtle finally found her size and started flipping through the rack for something suitably somber, she said, "Puddin, I don't have time for your foolishness today. I'm in a hurry."

"Goin' to that service, ain't ya?" asked Puddin, her small eyes gleaming in her pale face.

"If you're speaking about Victoria's, yes."

"You was at that party."

"You know I was," said Myrtle.

"Told you not to go."

"As if I listen to your nonsense, Puddin." She paused. The thing about Puddin, annoying as she was, is that she often did have information. This information was ordinarily passed along to Puddin by her cousin, the Efficient Bitsy.

"Look," said Myrtle. "I'll have a bit more time when I've shoved whatever I buy here into my washing machine. Why don't you come by my house shortly? We can chat."

Puddin looked suspicious, as if this was a new way to trap her into being productive. "Don't wanna clean."

"Don't worry, I won't ask you to do the job I pay you for," said Myrtle acidly.

But Puddin still looked mutinous.

"Just come along," said Myrtle. "We can both behave for a few minutes, surely."

"Okay." Then Puddin looked curious. "What're you gonna get to wear?"

Myrtle was pushing through the racks again. "Whatever is in my size. Apparently, there aren't a lot of big-boned, six-feet tall ladies in Bradley."

Puddin chortled at this, then narrowed her eyes as she took in the racks. "I'll help you."

"Will you?" Myrtle wasn't sure about this. Puddin wasn't exactly a fashionista. But then, neither was Myrtle. "All right. Let's divide and conquer."

Myrtle found a few demure black blouses. But they weren't her size.

"This one?" queried Puddin. She held up a rather hideous purple and yellow top with a sad-looking bow at its neck.

Myrtle shuddered, and Puddin kept shoveling through the blouses.

"We need something to go with my black slacks," said Myrtle. "The top I had was somehow torn."

"Well, that's gonna be easier than findin' pants for you. Yer tall."

"Yes, I know that. Thank you, Puddin."

Minutes later, Myrtle was despairing that she'd ever find something to wear to the blasted memorial service when Puddin crowed in glee. "Got it."

Myrtle turned as Puddin proudly presented a rather elegant white blouse with three-quarter sleeves. "Is it lined?" asked Myrtle, hardly daring to hope. "I'm not sure where my camisoles are."

"Yep."

Myrtle grabbed it from Puddin. "You've been quite unexpectedly helpful. A three-quarter sleeve is perfect for me. My arms are too long to get regular-sized sleeves. The blouse has to look as if it was designed to be shorter in length."

Puddin preened. "Saved your day."

"Indeed you did. All right, I'll buy this and meet you over at the house. Elaine and Jack are waiting outside for me."

Myrtle paid her $3.99 and hurriedly left the thrift shop with the blouse in tow. Elaine and Jack were waiting patiently in the parking lot. They cheered when Myrtle held up the plastic bag containing the blouse.

"Project successfully completed," said Elaine as they headed back toward Magnolia Lane.

"Yes. And you'll never believe who found the blouse."

Elaine said, "Not that woman who works there."

"Definitely not her. She's always too busy on her phone to be of any service to anyone. No, it was Puddin."

Elaine glanced quickly from the road to Myrtle, then back again. "You're kidding."

"No, indeed. She was lurking in the store, for reasons unknown. Puddin did find one monstrous blouse prior to this one, but then came up with a gem. So I'll throw it in the wash along with my funeral slacks as soon as I get home. Puddin's coming over to the house in a minute."

Elaine frowned. "To clean?"

"No, she was quite clear about not cleaning. We're going to have a conversation."

Elaine peered worriedly at Myrtle as if suspecting she'd suffered a mild stroke. "Puddin's coming over to visit."

"Correct."

"But Puddin stresses you out. Completely."

Myrtle said, "She certainly does. But she also often has unexpected information, mostly because her cousin Bitsy is something of a gossip. Besides, I have the feeling Puddin might know something about the case somehow."

"Surely Puddin wasn't part of Victoria's staff."

"Victoria had more sense than that. No, I think she might know something else. I'm just not sure what it is. She didn't want me to go to Victoria's party and seemed very leery about the house. I'd like to know just what's going through her head."

Minutes later, Myrtle's new, albeit used, white blouse was in the washing machine, along with her funeral slacks. To show her gratitude to Puddin, she pulled out a small bowl in the kitchen and filled it with potato chips from the trip she and Miles took to the grocery store. Soon, Puddin had let herself into the house.

"Have some chips," suggested Myrtle.

Puddin still seemed fairly suspicious that Myrtle was suddenly going to shove a mop and pail or a vacuum at her. "Okay."

They settled into seats in the living room. Puddin crunched on a few chips while Myrtle smiled at her and tried to appear innocuous. "Thanks for your help at the thrift store."

Puddin shrugged. "Weren't nuthin.'"

"Well, it was to me. I was in a real pickle. I wasn't going to have anything even vaguely appropriate to wear to the memorial service. You know how fancy Victoria's things always are. I'd imagine her brother would ensure the service would be up to Victoria's standards. And there I'd have been in a casual top with navy slacks. It simply wouldn't have done."

Puddin puffed up. "Yep. I knew as soon as I saw that top that it was gonna work." She chewed thoughtfully on a potato chip. "I tole you not to go to that party. That house is a bad place."

"Places aren't bad. *People* are bad."

Puddin shrugged. "Seems like both can be bad." She paused again. "Didn't you feel anything wrong in that place?"

"In Wisteria Hall? Certainly not. It was quite lovely inside."

Puddin tilted her head to one side. "What did she do to it? On the inside?"

"Why? Have you been in the house before?"

Puddin quickly said, "Nope. Jest wanted to know what it looked like now."

Myrtle gave an overview of the living room, the servants' passages, and the other things she'd seen on Victoria's tour. Then she described the conservatory.

"That ain't the conservatory. That's the mornin' room," said Puddin before she shut her mouth tight to keep more words from spilling out.

"Is it, now?" asked Myrtle. "That's a very interesting fun fact, Puddin."

"Jest guessin.'"

"I'm thinking not. I'm thinking you've been in that house before, Puddin. That you know it from a while back."

Puddin stood up. "I gotta run." She turned to leave, then turned around again to grab as many potato chips as she could before rushing to the door. She gave a small screech as Pasha bounded in as soon as the door was open. Then Puddin slammed the door behind her on her way out.

"Dear Pasha," said Myrtle as the black cat strode over and jumped into her lap. "I do believe Puddin has a secret."

Pasha's green eyes gleamed up at her in agreement.

Slightly over an hour later, the blouse and pants were clean and dry. The blouse, fortunately, hadn't seemed to get dingy-looking, despite having been washed with the black pants. Myrtle quickly changed and was ready right before Miles arrived. She was in his car before he'd even climbed out.

He gave her a bemused look. "New funeral clothes?"

"Just a new funeral top, actually. It's been quite an unusual day."

Miles said, "Considering it's still early, that's saying something."

"Puddin served as my personal shopper today. She found the blouse at the thrift store. Then she came back to my house for a snack of potato chips."

Miles said slowly, "That's quite unusual, for sure. You've struck up a friendship with Puddin?"

"Certainly not. Puddin is intolerable. You know that. But she can be helpful. And mysterious."

Miles looked as if he were trying and failing to picture a mysterious Puddin.

"She has some sort of past with Wisteria Hall. She wants to cover it up."

Miles frowned as he approached the church. "Wouldn't you know about that, if she *did* have a past with the house? You've been around longer than anyone else in this town."

"That's flagrant hyperbole yet again, Miles. There are plenty of people older than I am in Bradley. You can visit Greener Pastures Retirement Home and find a whole slew of them there."

Miles rolled his eyes. "Okay. Let me reword my statement. You've been around for a long time and appear to know a lot about Bradley's history. And, really, everyone in town."

"That's probably true. But I don't know everything there is to know. Especially if someone is keeping a secret under their hat. Maybe Puddin used to work there. It's all very interesting."

Miles pulled into a spot in front of the First Presbyterian Church. "I'm pleasantly surprised there's available parking."

"Remember, Victoria was a relative newcomer to Bradley. And the service is here at a church, not at the mansion. If her brother had held the service at Wisteria Hall, there'd have been tons of gawkers. There's clearly not the same interest in coming to First Pres."

The church was a solid brick Georgian Revival building from the 1920s with white columns and a modest steeple, built to last by a previous Bradley generation. It was the type of church that still felt adamant about using hymnals instead of projection screens and served coffee in actual china cups during fellowship time in the church hall.

Myrtle and Miles entered the sanctuary, sitting in a wooden pew. There was modest attendance, as the parking lot suggested. Myrtle saw that everyone who'd been at the party was present at the memorial service. Other people were possibly Victoria's business associates, neighbors, and curious locals.

"I wonder if that's her brother there," said Myrtle quietly.

Miles followed the direction of her gaze to a handsome man in his forties who looked tired and a bit anxious. He was holding papers in his hand. "It certainly looks as if he might be prepared to read a eulogy."

The service started right on time. The minister said all the appropriate funereal things, quoted the right verses, then spoke in abstract terms about Victoria. He appeared slightly relieved to be handing the pulpit over to the handsome man, who was indeed Victoria's brother.

Her brother spoke briefly about Victoria's "entrepreneurial spirit" and "business acumen." There were no personal stories about his sister, nor any fond words. As he closed, he cleared his throat. "Victoria would have loved to host you all at Wisteria Hall, but given recent events, we felt the church fellowship hall would be more appropriate."

Following a closing hymn, everyone headed over to the fellowship hall.

"I've always been rather intimidated by the church ladies here," confessed Miles in a low voice.

"You can't let them get to you. They'd take too much pleasure in that. Straighten your shoulders and look them right in the eye."

Miles did so, but the grimly efficient church ladies gave him a scornful gaze in response. He meekly asked for a scoop of chicken and broccoli casserole, a congealed salad, and a slice of pound cake. They sniffed as they deigned to provide them.

Myrtle lingered as she went through the line. She knew both of those scowling women. She knew also that they missed nothing going on around them. And that they were prone to gossip. So, while Miles was getting settled at a folding table covered with a white tablecloth, Myrtle was asking questions in an undertone.

"I didn't realize Victoria attended church here," she said to Franny Patterson.

Franny sniffed prodigiously. "She did *not*."

"I thought not. It was very generous of First Pres to hold the service, then," said Myrtle.

Winnifred, the old woman next to Franny, gave a croaking chuckle. "Not generous. It was quid pro quo."

"Ah. A little donation from Victoria?" asked Myrtle.

"A big donation from Victoria. I guess she didn't want to go to church, but she wanted to have some kind of pull here."

Franny intoned, "Twenty-five thousand dollars. Never saw her darken the doors of the church."

Winifred put in her two cents as she plopped some funeral ham on Myrtle's plate. "Money can't buy you into heaven, but it'll get you a church service."

Myrtle would have loitered longer in the casserole line, but there was a sudden rush of people getting seconds, so she moved reluctantly along to the sweet tea and lemonade corner, which was helmed by Mrs. Dupree and Mrs. Cole. Myrtle had no idea what their first names were, or if they even had them. They had seemed old even when she was a young woman, and must be exceedingly ancient now.

Fortunately, the beverage area was completely quiet. Even more fortunately, Mrs. Dupree and Mrs. Cole appeared to have run out of conversation with each other. They glommed onto Myrtle, eager to talk.

"Hi ladies," said Myrtle. "I'll have a sweet tea."

"How's everything going, Myrtle? I heard you were at Victoria's party," said Mrs. Dupree, pouring the tea into a glass.

"I was indeed," said Myrtle. Then she dutifully added, "Poor Victoria." She looked at Mrs. Cole. "As I recall, Victoria was a neighbor of yours, wasn't she?"

Mrs. Cole made a face. "She was. I wasn't delighted about that, of course. She had all sorts of renovation going on at Wisteria Hall. It could be quite noisy there."

Mrs. Dupree turned to Mrs. Cole. "Not just construction vehicles, either. You were telling me there were visitors at all hours. Or *one* visitor, at least."

Myrtle's ears perked up. "Is that so? Was Victoria seeing someone?" She suspected who it might be.

Mrs. Cole sniffed. "She was seeing someone, all right. But she was seeing someone who was already taken. You know how I feel about that."

Myrtle did indeed. Mrs. Cole's own husband had left her some years ago for a young waitress at Bo's Diner. Public opinion had gone heavily in Mrs. Cole's favor, and her ex-husband and the young waitress ended up fleeing Bradley for parts unknown. "Gracious," said Myrtle mildly. "Do you know who it was?"

Mrs. Cole had a satisfied look of someone who knew juicy gossip. "Mason Thornhill."

Myrtle hid a smile at being proven correct again. "Are you certain? He wasn't just there overseeing construction at Wisteria Hall? It was his company that was in charge of the renovation work."

"Yes, of course I *know* that. But he wouldn't have been conducting business over there at 9PM, would he?"

Myrtle said, "It does seem unlikely."

Mrs. Dupree chimed in, "Poor Ellie Thornhill. I wonder if she knew."

"Of course she knew," said Mrs. Cole immediately. "Wives always do."

The crowd from the casserole station finally made it to the sweet tea and lemonade corner, so Myrtle moved reluctantly away to join Miles at his table. He was pushing chicken and broccoli casserole around on his plate.

"Were you sleuthing over there?" asked Miles. "I can't imagine you were deliberately trying to engage in conversation with those dragon-ladies."

"They don't bite, Miles. I promise they're all quite innocuous. And yes, I was sleuthing. As usual, they all have their fingers on the pulse of the town. I discovered Victoria paid a significant donation to the church, although she never attended."

Miles swallowed down a glob of his congealed salad. "That seems par for the course for Victoria. She seemed to be the kind of person who wanted to be in a position of power and influence."

"Precisely. Then I went to the beverage table."

Miles looked enviously at Myrtle's sweet tea. "I missed that table."

"You must not have looked around very carefully. The church ladies will *always* serve sweet tea and lemonade. Anyway, I learned Victoria was having an affair with Mason. As I thought."

Miles looked startled, then glanced around to make sure no one was overhearing them. "Let's keep our voices down. That's pretty explosive stuff, especially at a memorial service."

"Isn't it?" Myrtle carefully cut up her funeral ham and stuck it into a fluffy biscuit to make a breakfast sandwich. "But then, I thought Mason seemed a bit shifty when we were talking to him outside Wisteria Hall, didn't you?"

Miles considered this. "I suppose I thought he might be holding something back. That he was perhaps not wanting to say that Victoria was difficult to work with. People don't like speaking ill of the dead sometimes. But I didn't think it was because Mason was having an affair with Victoria."

"It does make the plot thicken, doesn't it? Perhaps Mason wanted to move forward and Victoria wanted to break things off. Or maybe Victoria threatened to tell Ellie about the affair if Mason didn't continue it."

Miles said, "It gives Ellie more of a motive too. What if Ellie found out about the affair? She might have wanted to do away with Victoria. The party was the perfect opportunity to do that. When else would she have been in Wisteria Hall? It didn't seem as if she and Victoria were friends."

"Exactly. Look who Victoria invited. Adelaide, her hostile neighbor, Mason, her lover, and his wife. Tippy and Benton, who controlled her permits and zoning. Walter, whose inn she was destroying. She wasn't just playing cat-and mouse. She gathered all her enemies in one place, keeping them close."

"And she invited you and me," pointed out Miles.

"Well, you were a plus-one. But she invited me, knowing I was annoyed with her for stealing her yardman and for not receiving an invitation."

Miles said, "You don't know for a fact that Victoria was aware she'd taken Dusty away from you."

"I think Victoria knew a lot about what was going on around town. And that she liked playing games, as I mentioned before."

They were interrupted by Adelaide Monroe, wearing black and clutching her purse. "May I sit with the two of you?"

Chapter Sixteen

"Certainly," said Myrtle. Miles politely stood to pull out a chair for Adelaide.

She settled into the chair and put her purse down in the empty seat beside her.

"You're not eating?" asked Myrtle.

"Oh, I had a piece of pound cake earlier. To be honest, I'm not very hungry. This entire business had been truly awful. Have the police been talking to you, Myrtle?"

"As a matter of fact, they haven't." Myrtle was actually rather peeved by this. If you thought about it, she had something of a motive. She hadn't been pleased about Dusty's abduction. And she hadn't been pleased by the fact Victoria had neglected to invite her, but that was only because she'd thought Victoria was holding a big shindig, not an intimate gathering.

"Lucky," said Adelaide darkly. "You'd think your son would realize I'm not exactly a textbook killer."

Myrtle shrugged. "I have no influence over Red, as you well know. He does his own thing. And he's often quite irritating."

"Yes. I saw the gnomes."

"Adorable, aren't they?"

Adelaide carefully avoided answering the question.

Myrtle continued. "It must have been a very strange evening for you. Of course, the murder itself was startling."

"Murder?"

"Yes. The police are treating it as a suspicious death. You must have realized that, since they've come to speak to you, presumably after the party."

Adelaide looked very small in her seat. "I didn't ask."

Miles said sympathetically, "I'm sure it was also strange for you to see Wisteria Hall so different from how it had been when your family owned it."

"Yes, you're right about that. Howard Monroe built the mansion prior to the Civil War." Her voice was tight with emotion. "The Monroe family has served as guardians for the property for more than 150 years. It was a terrible shame when we had to sell it."

"It was an enormous home to maintain," said Miles quietly.

"Yes. It was far too much. I was initially happy for Victoria to have purchased the place. It seemed like she wanted to respect the history and preserve the feel of Wisteria Hall. My worst fear had been that someone would come in, raze the place, and build apartment buildings or some such." Adelaide shuddered.

"You said you were happy with Victoria's purchase at first. But you weren't later?" asked Myrtle.

"That's right. Although it wasn't an immediate thing. The renovations took their toll on my property, remember. You know about the flooding Victoria's landscaping caused. Some plants in my heritage garden were noted in Monroe family journals from the mid-1800s. I just can't seem to get over the damage. I warned Victoria in advance when she was getting that vile landscaping done that it was going to create problems."

Miles said slowly, "Surely you could have gotten the town to do some sort of environmental inspection."

Adelaide gave a short laugh. "That meeting was canceled after Victoria met with town officials. Then, whenever I attempted to complain to town council, they repeatedly tabled the discussion. And that's not all. There was all sorts of historical desecration occurring."

Myrtle lifted an eyebrow. "Like what?"

"There was a 150-year-old oak straddling our properties that was sawed down. I tell you, it was criminal. And you remember what the property *had* been called, Myrtle." Adelaide gave her a prompting look.

"Monroe Heights," said Myrtle obediently.

"Correct. She had the gall to change its name to Wisteria Hall. She effectively erased my family's history with the name change."

Myrtle said, "So you weren't particularly happy with Victoria, obviously."

Adelaide pressed her lips together. "No. No, I was not."

"Did you air your grievances to the police?"

Adelaide shook her head. "No, naturally. They'd have misinterpreted it completely. I know Red's your son, Myrtle, but I don't think he'd have understood that I could be angry but not act on it."

Myrtle thought Adelaide was selling Red short. He wasn't a stupid man. He also knew a good deal about human nature.

He'd have put two and two together and realized that Adelaide had quite a hefty motive.

But Adelaide continued her litany of wrongs. "That's not all. Victoria bragged about her 'Victorian Gothic experience' for guests. Complete with ghost stories about my family."

Myrtle quirked her eyebrow again. "Ghost stories?"

"Fabricated ones. She told me the Monroe family tragedy would be 'perfect for atmosphere.' She wanted to invent scandals, suicides, and other lurid nonsense to entertain tourists." Adelaide's voice trembled. "She was turning my ancestors into entertainment."

"Is the house haunted?"

"Certainly not!"

Myrtle said, "Is this why Victoria was so determined to have a séance?"

Adelaide gave a bitter laugh. "Market research, probably. See if her guests would pay extra for paranormal experiences. She mentioned it when I called to RSVP. She somehow thought I'd be flattered my family would be 'part of the mystique.'" Her voice dripped with contempt. "I told her what I thought of that idea."

Miles said quietly, "That must have been an uncomfortable conversation."

"Uncomfortable?" Adelaide's eyes flashed. "I hung up on her."

Myrtle could hear in Adelaide's tones the same indignation she'd hear when Adelaide was upbraiding one of her Latin students for not finishing his homework. "So Victoria's party was sort of a trial run. She wanted to test the waters to see how a séance would work."

"Apparently," huffed Adelaide. "Victoria mentioned something about planning on hiring your psychic friend full-time to do gigs there. Gigs!"

Myrtle had the feeling Wanda wouldn't have gone for that whatsoever. She also had the feeling Victoria would have put plenty of pressure on Wanda to force her to do whatever she wanted. Myrtle suddenly didn't feel very sorry that Victoria was dead. However, justice itself was still very important to Myrtle.

It was also important to Myrtle that she corner other suspects and speak with them again. A single interview with everyone wasn't enough. Mason, Walter, and Benton were also speaking with each other just a few feet from them as Ellie came up to join them. She'd like to learn more about what the other suspects might know.

But Adelaide still had something to say. "But I remembered something, Myrtle. Something important."

"About the murder?" Myrtle's eyes narrowed.

"That's right."

Myrtle said, "Then you must tell the police what you've learned. And tell me first."

"If I tell the police, they'll probably arrest the person. And I'm not completely convinced what I saw meant anything."

Myrtle was losing patience again. "You just said it was important."

"Yes, but who knows if I'm right or not? You see, it's about the nightshade," said Adelaide.

"How do you know it was nightshade?"

"Oh, it's obvious, isn't it? Anyway, if I'm right, it makes all the sense in the world." Then Adelaide looked worried. "But, if the police know that *I* knew about how to access the nightshade, that means they'd think I could have done it myself."

She was about to respond when Adelaide suddenly turned a shade paler than her already pale features. "I must go," she said quickly.

Myrtle turned to see what had spooked the old woman so much. That's when she saw Red sauntering up to her. She sighed. She'd much rather have spent her time speaking with other people of interest than with her son.

But she resigned herself to her fate. In fact, she rose to walk over and meet him. There was no point in subjecting Miles to her son. He was leery enough about getting on Red's bad side. Red looked cross, too, which was never a good sign. "Mama," he said in an ominous tone.

"For heaven's sake, Red. Your face is quite thunderous. What on earth is the problem?"

"You're the problem. You're at Victoria's memorial service, for one. I know the two of you weren't remotely close."

Myrtle pursed her lips, then said, "Perhaps Victoria thought we were close. After all, I was invited to her party. The least I could do was come to her service. Besides, funerals and memorial services are what counts as entertainment for the elderly in Bradley. That, and getting free samples at the Piggly Wiggly."

"You were also talking with Adelaide. One of my suspects."

"Well, I'm certainly glad to hear it confirmed that she *is* one of your suspects. I wasn't sure if you were falling down on the job. But she's not just a suspect. She's a former colleague of mine. As you might remember, since Adelaide Monroe taught you Latin," said Myrtle.

"A million years ago, yes."

"*Amo, amas amant* and so on."

Red rolled his eyes. "I didn't come over to conjugate verbs in Latin with you, Mama."

"See there! You remembered it was a verb. Well done, Adelaide. I always thought she was an excellent teacher."

Red seemed determined to get his point across. "Look, I don't want you being nosy. It's going to end badly if you do. Someone out there means business."

"Yes. You never want me being nosy. Let's acknowledge that to be the case and then move on." It was annoying speaking with Red when she could speak with other suspects. For instance, Mason and Ellie had now abandoned their discussion with the others and were sitting together at a table, tense and silent. Did Ellie know about Mason's affair with Victoria? Myrtle also saw Benton working the room like the politician he was. She wouldn't have minded having another conversation with him.

Red said, "There's more. Several people have brought up to me that you were very unhappy with Victoria. That you were angry that she'd hired Dusty and left your yard in such terrible shape. And you were angry that you hadn't originally gotten an invitation to her party. That you'd put her in the position of having to issue one."

"Busybodies."

Red said, "They're simply people letting me know that you're someone who should be considered a person of interest."

"You surely don't think I poisoned Victoria's teacup because I was upset about my yard. For heaven's sake, Red."

Red frowned. "That's something else. You seem to know a lot about the murder."

"How else could it have been perpetrated? Poison is the most likely option."

Red said, "And it's a weapon old women are traditionally fond of."

"Now you're just being ageist. I promise you I had nothing whatsoever to do with Victoria's death. Now, if you'll excuse me, I'm certain Miles is likely ready to go."

Miles was clearly ready to go. He was sitting at the table looking miserable as a couple of old ladies came up to coo at him. Church ladies were efficiently and grimly cleaning up.

"Be careful, Mama," Red said as she turned.

"I intend to be."

Chapter Seventeen

Myrtle walked back to the table, cane thumping as she went. She noticed most everyone else had already left.

"Ready to go?" asked Miles, a hopeful note in his voice.

"Yes. I think it's time."

They walked out of the fellowship hall and into the parking lot. Myrtle was deep in her thoughts, and Miles was quiet, too.

"Everything okay with Red?" he asked as they climbed into the car.

"Oh, it was just the usual nonsense about me keeping safe," said Myrtle breezily. "He threw in some extra stuff about my being a suspect."

"He surely can't believe that." Miles started up the car and drove cautiously out of the parking lot.

"Red just likes to get under my skin. You know that." Actually, Myrtle was rather relieved at finally being considered a suspect. It was annoying to be overlooked.

Miles said, "Red does indeed like to irritate you." He paused. "Let's get to the important part."

"What's the important part?"

"That Adelaide obviously knows who the killer is."

"Perhaps you should make a phone call, Miles. Although it's all very annoying. You know I'd usually prefer to keep this kind of information to myself. However, murderers do like to strike again, don't they? So this time, we'll let Red know. Or rather, *you* will. I'm not in the mood to speak with him right now."

Miles looked relieved. "Thank goodness. I wasn't going to sleep tonight."

"But right after you call, let's head over to Adelaide's. I want to finish our conversation. That way, I'll have the answer to the killer's identity before Red does." Myrtle beamed with satisfaction.

Miles said, "If I'm calling Red, I'll need to pull over to the side of the road to dial."

"For heaven's sake, Miles. I'll dial for you. Isn't your car on Bluetooth? You don't have to hold the phone, you know."

But Miles was adamant. "I don't feel right talking to a police officer while driving a motor vehicle. I'm certain that's unlawful."

So Miles pulled over, putting on his hazard lights. He carefully dialed Red's number and waited. He frowned. "No response."

"Leave a message for him. He's probably driving, himself."

Miles cleared his throat and carefully left a detailed message involving Adelaide's mysterious proclamation about nightshade. Then, looking relieved, he hung up.

"Now let's go to Adelaide's house," said Myrtle impatiently.

They set off in that direction. Miles said, "I wonder who's most likely to have access to nightshade."

"Oh, I'd think Adelaide, honestly. She's the one with the heirloom garden. But clearly, she's not implicating herself. Tippy would be another good choice. She has a tremendous garden. There must be some nightshade in there somewhere."

Miles looked scandalized. "Tippy? You can't think Tippy would have something to do with this."

"Why not? Tippy is a smart, determined, and organized woman. I think she could do anything she set her mind to."

"But Tippy isn't a *killer*."

Myrtle said, "Tippy would make an excellent killer. I don't know if she'd ever be caught. However, I think Benton would be a more likely candidate, if we're talking about nightshade from her yard."

They reached Adelaide's small home just minutes later. It was a beautiful property, although Myrtle could see the damage to the heirloom garden from the road. She clucked. "What a mess. No wonder Adelaide has been agitated about the flooding from Victoria's landscaping work."

They walked up a cobblestone path to the front door, which was slightly ajar. Myrtle frowned. "That doesn't seem like Adelaide. She's always been very security conscious."

Miles moved forward to hit the doorbell a few times.

"We should just walk in," said Myrtle.

Miles demurred. "She might be changing following the service."

There was no response at the doorbell. Miles rapped on the open door rather loudly. Nothing.

"Maybe she's working in her garden out back," suggested Myrtle. "She could have had her hands full of garden tools and couldn't shut the door the whole way."

Miles looked relieved at this explanation. They set off for the backyard.

"Oh, mercy," breathed Myrtle.

Because there was Adelaide Monroe, by her rose bed, a decorative stone next to her head.

Chapter Eighteen

Myrtle rushed over with Miles right behind her. But there was no pulse.

Miles was already on the phone, calling Red again. Getting no response, he dialed 911.

As he was carefully giving the dispatcher information and the address, Myrtle was sidling up to the decorative stone. It was some sort of memorial stone that said *In memory of Howard Monroe, builder of Monroe Heights.*

"How horrid," said Myrtle in an undertone. Adelaide appeared to have been struck from behind. She was still wearing her garden gloves, and her pruners were next to her. Myrtle was glad to see she likely hadn't known what was happening.

Miles hung up the phone. "They said police were on their way." He shook his head. "Poor Adelaide."

Myrtle was frowning. "This isn't just coincidental. Adelaide was telling us she knew who the killer was. Then she's suddenly struck down before she can say anything."

"The murderer couldn't have been sure she didn't say any-thing," said Miles slowly. He glanced around at the shrubs surrounding them as if someone could be about to leap out again with some other weapon.

"No, I suppose not. You're intimating that you and I might be the next victims."

Miles looked rather green at this thought.

Myrtle said slowly, "The problem is that the remainder of the suspects were all within earshot. Walter, Ellie, Mason, and Benton. Any of them could have tuned into our conversation with Adelaide and realized they'd been found out. Whoever it was didn't want to take the risk that she'd call the police. Or that she'd tell me later what she'd discovered. They left the service and headed straight over here to silence poor Adelaide."

They could hear a police siren in the distance. Miles sighed. "Red won't want us in the back yard. Let's go back near the car."

It was only a couple of minutes before Red and Perkins arrived together. Red's face was practically apoplectic, but Myrtle could tell that Perkins had been talking him down because he only shot a concerned look her way. Miles and Myrtle pointed toward the backyard, and the two policemen walked around the side of the house.

Perkins came back to speak with them first, which Myrtle was most grateful for. "Are the two of you okay?"

They nodded.

Perkins said gently, "Good. That must have been a horrible shock."

Myrtle said, "We were somewhat prepared, but only because the door was ajar when we arrived. It didn't really seem like something Adelaide would do. When she didn't answer the doorbell or Miles's knocking, we checked around back."

Perkins nodded. "Did you touch anything?"

Miles looked uncomfortable. "Well, the doorbell. And we pushed the door open a bit so that Myrtle could call for Adelaide. But that's it."

"We did try to find a pulse on Adelaide. But there wasn't one," added Myrtle.

Perkins said, "I see. What made the two of you decide to come by the house? Red was telling me in the car that Adelaide had just spoken with you both at the memorial service."

Miles was eager to absolve them of any wrongdoing. "Adelaide told us she remembered something about the nightshade. Maybe who might have access to it, or at least that's what we were speculating. When we left, I pulled over to the side of the road to call Red. I couldn't reach him, but I did leave a message."

Naturally, Miles had been very specific about where and when the call was made. He gave Myrtle a look, and she said, "I confirm Miles was on the side of the road. It was quite annoying, actually, because I wanted us to get to Adelaide's house as quickly as possible. We wanted to ask her more about the nightshade. Our conversation had been interrupted by Red."

Red was now walking back over to the front of the house, stringing crime scene tape as he went. Hearing his name, he glowered at Myrtle.

Perkins said in a soothing voice, "I see. Can you tell me if anyone overheard this conversation you were having?"

"Adelaide wasn't speaking very quietly."

Miles nodded. "I wondered if she thought Myrtle or I was hard of hearing."

Myrtle sighed, "Which is most annoying, of course, but also means that anyone could likely have heard her, even the church ladies cleaning up the casseroles. But yes, all your suspects were quite close to us at the time we were speaking with Adelaide. Any of them could have overheard and become alarmed."

Perkins said, "So you came straight here."

Miles interjected. "After stopping the car to make the call to Red. We found Adelaide, then called 911."

Red joined them, but was uncharacteristically quiet. Myrtle looked curiously at him. "Everything all right, Red?"

It was a leading question, and one that Red might ordinarily give a snarky response to. But this time he said, "Mama, you and Miles were probably just seconds behind the murderer. The killer could actually have still been on the scene."

Myrtle said defensively, "We did try reaching you, Red. Miles called to let you know what we'd heard from Adelaide."

"From the roadside," added Miles quickly.

Red said, "You should have told me at the service."

"You were steering that conversation onto my potential culpability," said Myrtle. "The subject went completely out of my mind until after you'd walked away."

Red sighed, rubbing the side of his face. "I was on a call when Miles tried phoning me. I can't help thinking how different things could have ended up."

"The murderer would have had a tough time killing both Miles *and* me. That would have taken some doing."

Red shook his head, clearly not wanting to think about how poorly it could have gone.

More police and a forensics team showed up. "Red and I need to go," said Perkins gently. "We'll be in touch if we need more information." With that, he and Red walked away to greet the other members of their team.

Miles and Myrtle were quiet as he drove back to Myrtle's house. Miles finally said, "That was all quite sudden."

"Yes. I don't know if I've ever been in a situation when someone was so quickly murdered after I've spoken with them. It's very unsettling. I may have to go inside and have a sherry. Although it's far before five."

"I think a sherry would be allowed, under the circumstances," said Miles. "I might even join you."

So it was, when Myrtle's doorbell rang an hour later, Tippy Chambers found her friends watching *Tomorrow's Promise* and sipping sherry. Both were facts Miles was rather horrified by.

Tippy was still wearing her dress from the memorial service. She looked rather shaken and very tired. "I heard about Adelaide."

"That was fast," said Myrtle, but without surprise. It was the way things operated in Bradley.

"Yes. One of her neighbors called me to fill me in. She knew Adelaide and I were friends." Tippy sighed. "I'm finding it hard to absorb. I just saw her at the service."

Myrtle waved at the sofa. "Please, have a seat, Tippy. Would you like some sherry? Miles and I were just indulging in a bit to calm our nerves."

Tippy opened her mouth as if she were about to say no. Then, on second thought, she said, "Actually, that would be lovely, Myrtle. I can fix it myself, though."

"No, no." There was absolutely no way that Myrtle was going to allow Tippy Chambers, hostess extraordinaire, to help herself to a glass of sherry. "I'll get it."

When she returned with the small sherry glass, Tippy was sitting on the sofa next to Miles. She blinked at the television screen. Is that *Tomorrow's Promise?*"

Miles was in an agony of embarrassment. He didn't like anyone to think that he watched soap operas. He didn't actually want anyone to think he even understood what a soap opera was. "Myrtle told me it would be something to take our mind off the murders." This was true, as a matter of fact.

Tippy nodded. "I totally agree. I'm quite a fan of the show, myself. My mother used to watch it back in the day. This whole thing with Luciano in the wine cellar is quite something, isn't it?"

Myrtle was delighted to find that the refined Tippy was such an avid viewer. She and Tippy had an animated conversation following that while Miles pretended not to know details about the storylines and characters.

Tippy said, "So are the two of you doing all right? I'm not so sure I am."

"It's quite a shock," said Myrtle dutifully. Tippy would expect nothing else.

"Yes, it is," agreed Miles, although he and Myrtle had been present at the discovery of numerous bodies in the past.

Tippy shook her head. "I just can't think who would possibly want to hurt Adelaide. She was such a sweet woman. She didn't do anything but putter in her garden."

Myrtle wanted to hear more about gardens in general. After all, nightshade and the access to it seemed to be a key component of the investigation. "She did have an amazing garden."

Tippy said hesitantly, "Am I to understand that you found her in her garden?"

Miles nodded solemnly. "At least she was doing something she enjoyed when she died."

Tippy sighed. "That's true. But still horrible. And she's had such a time lately."

"Has she?" asked Myrtle.

Tippy said, "Yes. I hate to speak ill of the dead, but Victoria had been providing Adelaide with a good deal of stress. Adelaide had some flooding that affected her garden and boathouse. Adelaide was also very concerned about having her old family home turned into a commercial enterprise."

Myrtle raised an eyebrow. "It's hardly as if it was becoming a grocery store or something. It was only going to be a bed-and-breakfast."

"Still, she felt very strongly about it. In fact, she'd been researching legal ways to block Victoria's permits."

Miles said slowly, "I can't imagine Victoria would have allowed that to happen."

"Probably not," agreed Tippy. "She was a very determined woman. Still, Adelaide had found some old covenant restrictions that might have applied, at least temporarily. She was planning to present her findings at the next town council meeting."

Myrtle said, "Tippy, you always know so much about the gardening world. I was thinking about growing some nightshade in my yard. I've always admired it."

"It's beautiful, but you'd have to keep an eye on little Jack. It's quite poisonous, you know."

Myrtle nodded. "So I understand. Of course I'd be very careful. I'd most like to get a mature plant, maybe one that's been divided from someone I know. Do you grow it?"

Tippy shook her head. "No."

"Do you know of anyone who does grow it?" asked Myrtle.

Tippy considered this. "I think Adelaide must have, although that's not particularly helpful, is it? I want to say that Ellie Thornhill does, too. She spoke about neighborhood gardens one week at garden club."

"Yes, I did enjoy that series. Sometimes it's wonderful to hear from botanists and extension agents of course, but hearing our neighbors talk about their own gardening challenges and successes was very meaningful."

"We'll have to do that again," said Tippy thoughtfully.

"So Ellie has nightshade," said Myrtle, just to get back to the original subject.

"That's right. Or, at least, she did when she gave the talk. You know, she's quite an interesting person with her pottery glazes and garden work. I'm sure she finds a lot of stress relief in those hobbies of hers."

Tippy sounded very much as if she might need some stress relief herself. Myrtle asked, "Is everything all right, Tippy?"

Tippy blinked furiously, immediately dispersing any tears that might have had the temerity to appear. Myrtle was relieved. She was never a fan of tears, although she couldn't imagine Tippy ever breaking down. She had too much of a handle on herself.

Actually, it might be a relief if she did, though. Tippy was a bit too superhuman for Myrtle's liking.

"Everything is fine," said Tippy brightly. "It's just been an awful week. But I'm not telling you anything you don't already know. The party was a nightmare. Then poor Adelaide. She and I were quite close."

Myrtle said, "I'm so sorry. Somehow, I hadn't realized that."

"Me either," said Miles.

Tippy gave them a determined smile. "I always checked in on her. After all, she was an older woman living by herself." She paused. "Not that you're *not* an older woman living by yourself, Myrtle. But somehow, Adelaide seemed more vulnerable."

Miles hid a smile. Myrtle was nearly six feet tall, armed with a cane, and her police chief son lived right across the street.

Myrtle inclined her head. "Yes, I'd agree with that. She was on her own more often, wasn't she?"

"That's right. She didn't have family in town. In fact, I'm not sure what family she might have had left. It was a source of some sorrow to her that she was the last of the Monroes. I think there are cousins somewhere." Tippy looked thoughtful. "Perhaps I'm the one who should give the memorial service."

"That would be a lovely way to remember Adelaide," said Myrtle. She was quiet for a few moments, then said, "You know how I despise gossip."

But Tippy didn't seem to know this. In fact, Tippy gave Myrtle a wry look in response. "Of course you do."

"I couldn't help but overhear something rather disturbing at Victoria's service. I understand Mason might have been having an affair."

Tippy frowned. "Really? But Mason and Ellie seem like such a wonderful couple. I hate to hear that. Are you sure it's true?"

"Well, no, naturally. That's the nature of gossip, isn't it?"

Tippy said, "Did they say who they thought Mason was having the affair with?"

"Victoria."

"Ohhh," said Tippy. She was quiet for a few moments.

Miles cleared his throat. "Maybe nothing happened at all." He seemed to try to make Tippy feel better. Tippy did seem rather sad about the news. Maybe it was just a matter of the straw breaking the camel's back. It had been a long week, after all.

Tippy said, "Actually, now that I think about it, I believe the gossip might have some merit. I went by to see Victoria one day a couple of weeks ago. I'd run into her at the grocery store, and she'd given me an open invitation to drop by and see the renovations. You know that Benton and I spent so much time researching historically-appropriate renovations when we remodeled our house."

Myrtle wasn't surprised to hear this at all. Tippy was constantly in the process of making over her own historic home. And she never did anything halfway.

Tippy continued, "Anyway, I dropped by. Mason's van was there, but that was hardly a surprise as he was the one supervising the entire operation. I rapped on the front door, but there wasn't an answer. So I rang the doorbell. I was about to leave, when Victoria finally came to the door."

"Not in *dishabille*?" asked Myrtle.

Miles looked as if he were prepared to be scandalized.

"No, she was fully-clothed," said Tippy slowly. "But I did get the sense I'd interrupted something. Victoria's hair was quite mussed-up, and she quickly apologized, saying it wasn't a good time. Said something about a headache, I believe. Then she told me I'd be on the guest list for an upcoming party she was planning and she'd give a tour then. I never did see Mason."

Myrtle said, "That certainly does sound as if you'd interrupted something."

"Yes. Poor Ellie."

Miles asked, "Do you think Ellie knows?"

Tippy frowned at this, thinking. "Well, it's possible. She hasn't been herself lately. I noticed at the party that she seemed a bit off. Very quiet. I thought maybe she and Mason had had a tiff right before arriving at Wisteria Hall." She shook her head. "Goodness. It really has been a week."

Then she gracefully stood up. "I'd better be on my way. Benton will wonder where I am. And I'll be in touch about the memorial service. After all, someone needs to handle the arrangements. Maybe we should think about collecting old photos of Adelaide with friends for a memorial table." She leaned over and hugged Myrtle and a surprised Miles. "Please be careful, both of you"

Miles saw her out then returned to join Myrtle. "What do you make of all that?"

"It seems both Adelaide and Ellie had access to nightshade. Naturally, I'm thinking Adelaide wasn't the one who murdered Victoria, even though she had plenty of motive. It's unlikely we'd have two separate killers running around Bradley at once."

"It's happened before," pointed out Miles in a morose tone.

"Indeed. But it doesn't seem right this time. Ellie does have an excellent motive to murder Victoria. Victoria was a threat to her marriage. And Tippy is certainly someone who picks up on undertones. I believe her when she says she thought there was tension between Mason and Ellie at the party. Plus, I saw the two of them sitting quietly at a table by themselves at the memorial service."

Miles said, "Lots of married couples don't have much to say to each other."

"True. But again, it seemed as if they were at odds. No, I think Ellie is completely aware of Mason's affair. And she has access to nightshade."

Miles asked, "And Adelaide?"

"Adelaide might have seen Ellie lingering near Victoria's teacup. Then Ellie would have had to eliminate her."

"Wouldn't Adelaide have said something?" asked Miles. "I mean, directly after it happened? Why would she have waited and gotten herself killed?"

"Oh, there are plenty of reasons why she wouldn't have. For one, the police stubbornly weren't calling it murder or even a suspicious death at first. By the time they did, perhaps Adelaide started reconsidering what she'd seen. Also, she might not have wanted to implicate Ellie. Maybe she wanted to speak with Ellie first and make sure there wasn't a reasonable explanation."

Miles said, "A reasonable explanation for someone putting a substance in a teacup?"

"I'm not saying it makes any sense, I'm just saying it could be what Adelaide was thinking."

Miles said, "It's all very convoluted."

"No, it's really not, Miles. It's fairly simple because it's limited to people at that wretched party. Excluding you, Wanda, and me, that's Tippy and Benton, Mason and Ellie, Adelaide, and Walter. They all have fairly good motives."

"Even Tippy?" asked Miles, sounding doubtful.

"I wouldn't put anything past Tippy, although I do think it sounds unlikely." She paused. "I notice you didn't mention Benton as being above suspicion."

Miles said, "I might be biased against Benton. I've never really been at ease around him."

"Yes, I understand that. He seems to have a certain disdain for other people, doesn't he? It's unusual in a politician. I think the only reason he's done so well in the political arena is because of his networking. He's not disdainful toward people who help him promote his agenda. I could see him knocking out someone who was causing him issues."

"Like Victoria," said Miles. "What issues are we thinking she caused him, again?"

"Well, she seemed to be practically forcing him into helping her with her zoning issues. Benton was likely also having to pressure Tippy, too, since she was the swing vote. Maybe Benton didn't enjoy being put in that position and decided to rid himself of the trouble." She paused. "Of course, Benton has never been particularly faithful to poor Tippy. Maybe Victoria was blackmailing Benton to approve her permit requests."

Miles sighed. "I suppose so. What are our next steps? We're done for the day, aren't we?"

"Oh, I think so. But I believe we're due for another chat with Mason and Walter. Perhaps we can seek them out tomorrow. Let's get an early start. Perhaps another breakfast at Bo's Diner is in order."

Miles said, "You seem to have more of an appetite in the morning than I do."

"Your stomach is quite a delicate organ. I'm ravenous at least three times a day, if not more. Shall we say seven o'clock?"

Miles nodded. This decided, they settled back to watch the rest of *Tomorrow's Promise*. Luciano had apparently survived his so-called fatal boating accident. The plot shift required lots of attention, and Myrtle and Miles happily devoted themselves to it.

Chapter Nineteen

Myrtle was ready when Miles pulled the car up at seven the next morning.

"Did you sleep well?" She buckled her seatbelt as Miles cautiously backed up the car.

"I did. But you seemed to have been up working. I saw the newspaper this morning. Your story was on the front page."

Myrtle beamed at this. "Yes. But there was no need to stay up late to make the paper. After you left yesterday afternoon, I had plenty of time to get the story over to Sloan. Wasn't it well-written?"

"I'd expect nothing less."

Bo's Diner was surprisingly busy. This morning, there were plenty of people who'd apparently stopped by for breakfast before heading to work.

"Mercy," said Myrtle. "It's crowded." She scanned the diner before smiling. "Walter Beaumont is here."

"We're not going to sit down with him, are we?" Miles looked alarmed.

"Why not? There's plenty of room at his booth. And I've just done him a tremendous favor by writing up a story about his family inn."

Miles said, "Which hasn't run yet."

"True. I'll have to push Sloan on that. I can't help the fact that people keep being murdered in town, though. Naturally, that affects what runs in the paper." She frowned at him. "Don't dither, Miles. It'll be fine."

Miles trailed behind her as Myrtle headed with purpose to Walter's booth.

"May we join you?" she asked Walter pleasantly.

He was startled, not expecting to share his table with anyone. "Miss Myrtle. Okay. Why not?"

Miles gave him an apologetic look as he and Myrtle settled in and ordered coffee. Then Miles buried his face in his laminated menu as if he'd never seen the options before. As if he wasn't already planning on ordering oatmeal.

Walter cleared his throat. "I heard someone mention you and Miles were on the scene when Adelaide was discovered. That must have been terrible."

"It was. Yes, Miles and I were the ones who found her and called the authorities. It was most horrid. Poor Adelaide. And we'd just seen her at the memorial service."

Walter nodded sadly. "Was it—well, do you think she suffered?"

"I certainly hope not. I don't think she did, do you, Miles?"

Miles, thus summoned from his scrutiny of the menu, popped his head up. "No, I don't believe she did. She likely never knew what hit her."

"I'm glad to hear it," said Walter, sounding relieved. "I'd hate to think that she was afraid or that she died slowly."

"It doesn't seem like it," said Myrtle. She paused. "You were friends with Adelaide, then?"

"I wouldn't necessarily call us *friends*, but we were very friendly with each other. After all, both our families were prominent in the town. Lots of Bradley history is entwined with both the Monroe and Beaumont families. We were cousins somewhere down the line, too."

This didn't surprise Myrtle at all. Bradley was a small enough town that nearly everyone who'd had a family presence there for generations was related somehow.

"Did you go back to the inn after the service?" asked Myrtle sweetly. "Or did you go for a drive?"

"Oh, I went back to the inn. I think I've mentioned that we've had a staffing problem lately. I had someone watching the front desk, but I couldn't keep them waiting for long. Besides, I needed to work on the books." Walter looked as if working on the books wasn't his favorite task.

"Is everything going well at work?" asked Myrtle, looking solicitous. "I'd hate it if we lost The Bradley Inn. It's an institution."

Walter brightened at this. "It is, isn't it? And I do appreciate the feature the paper is running on it."

"Yes, Miles and I were just talking about the feature a few minutes ago. I'm sorry it hasn't been published yet, but Sloan has been busy with articles on the murders, of course. I'm sure it'll print soon."

Walter nodded. "It's very appreciated. And, to answer your question, business has picked up just slightly. I'm sure October will be a good month for us, though. It usually is, because we have tourists coming in to see the fall leaves. That should help us out a bit."

Myrtle said, "I'd imagine that, in some aspects, you'll be relieved not to have the competition from Victoria. The bed-and-breakfast will have to be jettisoned, I'm guessing. Unless she has family who want to take the idea and run with it. That brother of hers, for instance."

"Actually, I spoke with her brother at the memorial service. It was all a bit awkward, of course, but after expressing my condolences, I did ask if he had plans for continuing along with Victoria's bed-and-breakfast concept. He said he didn't and that he was planning on selling the property at the first opportunity. I believe he wanted to make sure all the renovations were completed first, however." Walter looked very pleased.

"I see. Well, that's good news for the inn. Are you getting your housekeeper back? Brenda, wasn't it?"

Walter finished chewing some of his omelet. "Yes. I can't tell you how delighted I was. Of course, Brenda was a bit sheepish at having left in the first place, but I told her bygones were bygones. I did feel bad that I couldn't offer to pay her what Victoria was giving her, but she understood that. It's not from lack of wanting to, I assured her. A good housekeeper is worth her weight in gold."

The waitress came by to get their orders. Myrtle ordered a three-egg breakfast with hash browns and rye toast. Miles, as expected, got his customary oatmeal.

Myrtle said, "Thinking back to Adelaide. Who do you suspect might have wanted to do her harm?"

"I've no idea, Miss Myrtle."

Myrtle said with a hint of impatience, "If you had to speculate, though."

Walter considered this. "Well, as I'd mentioned before, I think Benton could do it. He must have gotten tired of having to be at Victoria's beck and call on the planning commission. But why he'd have wanted to eliminate Adelaide? I've simply no idea."

Miles said, "Maybe Adelaide was a witness to something?"

Walter looked at Miles with surprise, as if he hadn't remembered he was there. "Yes, I suppose you're right. Adelaide might have noticed something at the party and mentioned it to Benton. Then Benton would have had to kill her to keep her quiet." He held up his hands. "Not that I'm suggesting Benton did it, mind you."

"Of course not," said Myrtle smoothly.

"Poor Adelaide," said Walter again. He sighed. "I remember our families having get-togethers from time-to-time when I was growing up. My parents thought very highly of her parents. The Monroes were always so important to Bradley. Now, they're all gone. No more Monroes in Bradley. It's just so difficult to wrap my head around. And one day, it'll be the same for my family. The Beaumonts."

Miles said, "Maybe your children will change their minds about returning to Bradley. When it comes down to it, they may realize the inn and the family history is more important to them than they thought."

Walter gave him a sad look. "I'd like to believe that. But it sure doesn't seem that way. They're both off in big cities. They have their own families and jobs there. I can't really see them giving it all up to return to Bradley to run a struggling inn."

With this, Walter stood up. "It was good seeing you both. I should run get back to the inn. Hope you'll have a good day."

After he left, Myrtle and Miles's food arrived at the table. They ate it quietly, mulling over their conversation with Walter.

"He does seem happy that the inn is doing better," said Myrtle. "Now he has Brenda back and other staff members. He won't have the competition from Wisteria Hall. It all worked out very well for him."

Miles nodded, pushing his oatmeal around in his bowl. "Do you think he could have done it? Poisoned Victoria and killed Adelaide?"

"I don't think we should underestimate him. He seems quite invested in not wanting to let his ancestors down. It's a lot of responsibility, and it seems to have weighed on him. Now, it's like a tremendous burden has lifted."

Miles said, "It was rather fortuitous that we could speak with him over breakfast. I wasn't looking forward to figuring out how to meet with him again without it looking contrived."

"Yes. We probably won't have the same luck with Mason. We'll likely have to chase him down."

Miles's face dropped at this. "We can't think of anything that needs constructing?"

"No. We don't want to go down that road, Miles. Mason is a salesman at heart. He'd never leave us alone. We'd be forever talking about the fictitious project we were lying about. No, it's best to just search him out. Beard the lion in his den."

Miles didn't appear to appreciate this direct approach. "Let's think of something. I'll work on it."

"You do that. Regardless, it's still too early in the day to hunt down Mason. We'll go back to my house and regroup a while. Then we'll do some driving around, unless you come up with a better plan."

Thirty minutes later, they were back at Myrtle's house. Miles said, "Your yard does look a lot better."

"Doesn't it? Of course, Red had the temerity to suggest I might be a culprit in Victoria's death because she stole Dusty from me." Myrtle huffed. "He knows just how to get under my skin."

They got out of the car. Miles said, "It's a fairly valid motive, though. Somewhat similar to Walter's. Walter was upset because Victoria was poaching his staff. You were angry because she'd lured Dusty away."

"Yes, but Dusty wasn't a full-time employee." She paused as they walked into her house. "There's something I wanted to tell you, but I keep forgetting. Puddin has been quite mysterious lately."

"Somehow, I can't picture that. Puddin doesn't seem like someone with secrets. In fact, she sort of lays it all out there."

"I know," said Myrtle. "Luckily, she does a very poor job *keeping* secrets. She has a lot of knowledge about Wisteria Hall."

"Maybe she's been in there before. She might have had to help out with the cleaning once or twice if the regular housekeeper couldn't make it. I'm sure there are reasonable explanations."

"Miles, I'm telling you, it's very odd. Puddin will say she hasn't been in the house, but then she'll make statements where it's completely obvious she has. She gave some kind of observation about the conservatory being the morning room and stuff like that. I'm going to have to get to the bottom of it."

"I can't see how you're going to do that," said Miles. "Puddin isn't the kind of person who'd react well to being pushed for information. She'd just shut down."

"I think she'll give it all up if we seek her out and pressure her."

"Let's not. I'm pretty sure I don't have the patience for Puddin this morning. In fact, I'm feeling rather sleepy after a big bowl of oatmeal," said Miles.

"You didn't even finish the oatmeal!"

Miles said, "But I ate until I was stuffed. I did remind you that I don't have much appetite in the mornings."

"I'll drive then. This is the perfect time. Puddin will still be at home, looking for reasons not to go work. Piddling around."

"What excuse can we possibly have?" asked Miles.

"We don't need an excuse. It's Puddin. We'll just show up. Car keys?"

Miles pressed his lips together.

"For heaven's sake. I'm an excellent driver. You're well-aware of this. We'll just set out on a nice little drive."

Miles seemed to realize Myrtle wouldn't stop. He sighed and handed over the keys.

Minutes later, Myrtle was driving Miles down the road at the sedate speed of fifteen miles an hour. Her hands gripped the steering wheel at ten and two, and she sat straight in her seat, eyes focused ahead of her.

"Hopefully we'll make it to Puddin's before lunchtime," said Miles in an undertone.

"What was that? You're muttering again."

"Nothing."

Myrtle said, "Just close your eyes and take a nap. You'll probably feel much better."

"I don't think closing my eyes would make me feel at all better."

Someone behind Myrtle started honking their horn.

"What is wrong with people?" growled Myrtle.

"They must be trying to get to work on time."

Myrtle said, "Then they should have set out sooner. It's their own fault, not mine."

"You're going slower than the speed limit."

"Yes," said Myrtle, "but that's why it's called a speed *limit*. It indicates no one is supposed to go over that. I thought you understood this, Miles."

"Not everyone views speed limits that way."

Myrtle said, "The speed limit's not a *suggestion*. No wonder Red has to write so many tickets."

"I think Red writes so many tickets because he rarely has anything else going on. It's usually either feast or famine in Bradley. Murder or speeding tickets."

Puddin's house was a modest affair with an unkempt yard and, at least during past visits, an equally unkempt inside. Both vehicles were outside.

"They're home," said Myrtle with satisfaction as she parked the car.

Miles said, "Maybe I should stay in the car."

"Maybe you should. You look so very uncomfortable. Perhaps if you take a small nap, you'll feel better. I'll roll down the windows."

After doing so, Myrtle trudged down an overgrown walkway to the front door. She rang the doorbell but could hear no discernible sound from inside. She pounded on the door.

Chapter Twenty

Dusty exclaimed from inside the house, then the front door flew open. He gaped at her. He was in a very old-fashioned pair of pajamas. "I done mowed!"

"I know you did. I just decided to drop by for a little visit."

"It's early!" howled Dusty.

"It's early on the west coast of the US. However, we're in the Eastern time zone. It's not at all early. Early is when I got up this morning."

Dusty's mouth flapped open and closed, but no words came out.

"I'd like to see Puddin, if she's available." Myrtle moved toward the door, and Dusty automatically got out of her way.

"I gotta git ready fer work," muttered Dusty, heading off for the back of the house.

Myrtle scanned the untidy living room to see if she could find Puddin. Her first choice was to look in front of the television, since Puddin was always an avid viewer. But she wasn't there.

She heard Dusty hollering for Puddin in the back. Puddin seemed to be arguing with Dusty about whether she had a responsibility to speak with Myrtle at all.

Myrtle took the opportunity to take a bit of a tour through Puddin's living room. She peered at a picture that seemed to be a selfie of Puddin and Dusty in bathing suits at Myrtle Beach with cups of beer in their hands.

There was another picture on the wall, this one in an old frame. Myrtle's eyes opened wide. It was clearly Wisteria Hall. There were women in old-fashioned dresses and hats standing on the front steps for a group photo.

Dusty unhappily showed up again. "Dudn't wanna come out."

"I'm sure she'll want to speak with me. Perhaps she just needs a minute to get dressed." She paused. "I'm curious about this photo."

Dusty sidled up to the framed picture, squinting as if he'd never noticed it before. "Her great-grandma or somethin's in it."

"*Is* she now?" Myrtle carefully removed the photograph from the wall, checking the back. Helpfully, some forebear of Puddin's had identified the women in the picture and circled the name of the family member in question.

"Tell Puddin I'd like to speak with her about Wisteria Hall."

Dusty stomped off to relay the message loudly to his wife. As expected, Puddin came immediately out.

"Whatcha doin' here?" she hissed. "You goin' through my stuff?"

"I'm trying to glean more information about my housekeeper since she hasn't been very forthcoming," said Myrtle. "Am I to understand you're related to the original owners of Wisteria Hall? The Monroes?"

Puddin said, "Am not!"

"Dusty already confirmed it."

Puddin shot her husband a death glare. Dusty took the opportunity to quietly disappear.

"Was your mother a Monroe?"

"Nope," said Puddin between gritted teeth.

"So your connection was farther down the line, then. Grandmother? Great-grandmother?"

"Great," confirmed Puddin sullenly.

"So you're . . . what? A cousin of Adelaide's?"

"Distant!" insisted Puddin.

"Why on earth would you want to conceal such a connection?"

Puddin heaved out a great sigh. "Didn't want nobody knowin'. People treat you different."

"Clearly, you must have spent some time there. You remembered all the rooms and what they looked like. You seemed put-out by Victoria's renovations."

"Felt wrong, Victoria changin' everything."

Myrtle frowned. "You'd mentioned previously that it was a bad house. You warned me against going there."

"An' you went anyway!"

"Yes," said Myrtle. "Because you didn't provide any context. What makes you think it was such a bad place?"

"It is!"

Myrtle tried to summon her escaping patience. "But why?"

"Bad luck over there. The family done lost everything and hadta sell up. My grandma cried a lot over it."

"So you have some bad memories. That doesn't mean the house itself is bad," said Myrtle.

"Is too! An' my cousins told me about the ghosts there. Said the house remembered everythin'. An' didn't like strangers. Like you."

Myrtle said, "Your cousins were just messing with you, Puddin, the way cousins do. Were you the youngest?"

Puddin nodded her head, still looking resentful.

"I'm sure they made everything up. At any rate, you should be proud of your family heritage. The Monroes have always been an important family in Bradley." She paused. "I'm surprised I didn't know anything about this. But then, I guess I wasn't acquainted with you until later in your life, so no wonder."

Dusty resurfaced from the back, now wearing his work clothes. He apparently overheard part of their conversation because he walked to a cabinet and pulled out an old Bible, thrusting it at Myrtle while Puddin glowered at him.

"A family Bible," said Myrtle, opening the front of the book carefully. There was Puddin's family tree. It had indeed taken some surprising divergences. "So you grew up going to Wisteria Hall. What a surprising thing to remain silent about."

Puddin's chin was up, a sure sign she was feeling defensive. "Momma and daddy didn't wanna talk about it."

"Why on earth not? I'd think they'd be proud of your mom's heritage. And yours. Why, you're a local aristocrat, Puddin!"

But Puddin didn't seem very pleased by this fact. "They were ashamed they lost the money. Seemed better just not to say nuthin' about it."

"An interesting take. You must have enjoyed *something* about the house, though. Playing hide and seek, maybe?"

Puddin made a face. "Scary. My cousins would pop in and out of hidden passages and secret rooms. Scared me half to death."

"Well, I think it all adds another layer of complexity to you. The more I think I understand you, the less I do."

Puddin seemed to like this idea. She puffed up. "Yep. Hard to know me."

Myrtle said, "Did you ever meet Victoria?"

"Nope. Wanted nuthin' to do with her."

Myrtle said, "I'd imagine you weren't too pleased to have Dusty working there, then."

"Nope," said Puddin again, this time with more feeling. "Tole him that. Didn't listen."

"Yes, that's a common theme when it comes to Dusty."

"Hey!" came a bellow from another room. Dusty appeared to disagree with this characterization. Puddin and Myrtle shared a smile.

A minute later, Myrtle was back in the car with Miles. He'd indeed fallen asleep and startled awake when she closed the driver-side door.

"All good?" he asked in a bleary voice.

"Yes. At least one mystery is cleared up."

Miles rubbed his eyes and fastened his seatbelt again as Myrtle slowly drove away. "Puddin came clean?"

"Not until I found a family Bible with a family tree in it. It seems Puddin is a Monroe."

This had the effect of immediately waking up Miles. "No way."

"It's true."

Myrtle set off driving, peering ahead of her with concentration. Miles quietly let her drive, not wanting to distract her. He was also trying to grasp this new, surprising information. When Myrtle had successfully made several turns of the car and was on a straight path, he said, "I'm surprised Puddin hasn't been bragging about it to all and sundry."

"I know. That was my first thought, too. Puddin is insufferable when she has something to brag about. She went on and on about winning stamps at the bingo the VFW put on."

Miles said, "So why wouldn't she do the same for being part of the Monroe family?"

"Apparently, her family was ashamed by their fall from grace. They preferred to cover it up instead of talking about it. Puddin fell into line. Also, her father was decidedly *not* a Monroe. I suppose his influence made the most impact on her."

Miles raised his eyebrows. "This case is full of surprises."

"And we're not done yet. Let's see what Ellie knows."

Miles was horrified. "Ellie! I thought we were going to see Mason."

"Well, now I want to see Ellie. I have the feeling she knows all about Mason's dalliance with Victoria."

Miles was even more horrified. "We can't say anything to her about it. Myrtle! She may not know. We'll wreck a marriage."

"Mason isn't being at all circumspect about wrecking his marriage. He's the one to blame, not us. Besides, I'll be tactful. You know me; I'm the soul of tact."

Miles said, "I *don't* know that. In fact, you're often a lot blunter than you think you are."

"Sometimes that's the only way to get information. Besides, at my age, you can get away with everything. Don't worry, I have a good reason to run by and see Ellie."

Miles didn't seem very relieved at this news. "What's the reason?"

"I want to see her pottery studio. Creating pottery would make for an excellent hobby."

Miles scowled. "You're taking up pottery? That seems rather contrived, Myrtle."

"Are you saying I can't grow as I age? I wouldn't have thought you'd be ageist."

Miles said, "I'm just saying I can't see you as a potter."

Myrtle sniffed. "As a matter of fact, I was planning on recommending it as a pastime for Elaine. I believe she tried it once before, but she should take it up again. After all, the rooster thing doesn't seem to be working out. That chicken is violent. I predict Scotty will end up at a place in the country before long."

Miles now looked pleased. "That's actually a good idea. I've been terrified to get my mail the last few days."

Chapter Twenty-One

Soon they were at Mason and Ellie's house. It was a modern home with a separate building in the back. There was a well-maintained herb and flower garden flanking the path to the studio. Myrtle could see little markers identifying the various plants.

When they got out of the car, they heard lively music coming from the small building. "I think she must be in there working," said Myrtle.

Miles hesitated. "I hate surprising her."

"We'll give plenty of indication that we're approaching."

And indeed, Myrtle started calling Ellie from yards away. "Ellie? Yoo-hoo! It's Miles and Myrtle."

"That wasn't scary at all," said Miles.

"Sarcasm from you, Miles? I'm surprised."

Ellie greeted them at the door with a smile. She was wearing a clay-stained apron. "Well, hello, you two. Thanks for dropping by. Want to see the studio?"

"I'd love to," said Myrtle.

"We're not disturbing you, are we?" asked Miles with concern.

"I've just finished with a pot, so this is a good time. Come on in."

Myrtle looked around the building. "This must have been a detached garage at some point."

"Exactly. It was a two-car garage, which was perfect. Mason converted it into a workspace for me."

Miles said, "It must be nice to get this much natural light."

"It is. That's something else Mason made sure of. The windows are all added, of course. The garage didn't have any at first."

Myrtle took in a potter's wheel, a worktable with various tools hung on a pegboard, and buckets of clay scraps.

Ellie said apologetically, "I'm afraid I only have stools to sit on. Nothing with a back on it. Is that all right?"

"Oh, we're good to stand. We just wanted to see your space. My daughter-in-law, Elaine, is a sweet woman but has the most horrid hobbies. Wouldn't you agree, Miles?"

Miles nodded soberly to confirm this.

"I'd love to direct her into pottery," continued Myrtle. "Do you ever teach classes or anything?"

Ellie said, "Sometimes, but just a one-on-one class. Since I do this full-time, there isn't much opportunity to teach. I'm constantly filling special orders from both individuals and businesses."

"I had no idea you had such a successful enterprise," said Myrtle. "Congratulations. You've clearly put in a lot of hard work." She paused. "Don't I also remember your saying you helped with the books for Thornhill Construction?"

Ellie gave them a wry look. "Yes. That would be my other full-time job. It keeps me busy."

"I'd say."

Ellie frowned. "Didn't I hear that the two of you discovered poor Adelaide? She's been constantly in the back of my mind. It's a wonder I've been able to focus on my work at all. Finding her must have been horrible."

"Oh, it was. Of course, we'd just seen her at the memorial service. Such a terrible thing," clucked Myrtle. She'd found it was often better to slip into innocuous-old-lady mode in order to elicit more information.

"You poor thing. I'm sure you and Adelaide must have known each other for a long while," said Ellie sympathetically.

"Yes indeed. She and I both taught together, years ago. I taught English and she, Latin. It was quite a time." Myrtle affected a reminiscent look.

"Well, I was very sorry to hear the news. I didn't know Adelaide well, but she seemed like a wonderful person. I wish I'd gotten to know her better."

Myrtle sweetly asked, "I suppose you went home right after the memorial? It was so good of you to attend Victoria's service."

"I did head right to the house," said Ellie. "I'd wanted to get some more work done in the studio before Mason had me balancing the books again."

Myrtle said, "You and Mason seem like quite a team."

Which is when Ellie, completely out of the blue, burst into noisy tears.

Miles hurriedly pulled out a carefully pressed and perfectly clean handkerchief from his pocket, glaring at Myrtle as he passed it to Ellie. Myrtle gave a slight shrug. After all, she'd said nothing to cause such an uproar. Miles, however, didn't seem to view it that way.

"I'm so sorry," gasped Ellie minutes later. Myrtle had been patting her back and saying, "there, there."

Myrtle was vastly relieved Ellie seemed to gain control of herself. "Oh heavens, Ellie. You simply mustn't apologize. It's been a terribly hard week, hasn't it? Truly dreadful. Of course you must feel overwhelmed."

Miles made a strangled sound of agreement.

Ellie was hiccupping now.

"Can I get you a glass of water?" asked Miles, practically leaping to his feet. "You need water. Where's your kitchen? Never mind, I'll find it." He fled before anyone could stop him.

Myrtle said, "Are you sure you're all right? Is there anything I can do?" Then she winced as her concern seemed to make Ellie cry again.

Ellie scrubbed her tears away with Miles's handkerchief. "No, there's really nothing anyone can do. I found out Mason was having an affair with Victoria. And you're right—I thought he and I made an amazing team. But apparently, we're not."

Myrtle said, "I'm so sorry to hear it. That must be so very distressing."

"It is. I haven't known what to do about it. Plus, I just feel so totally humiliated. I had no idea and now I feel like the whole town of Bradley was aware of it and feeling sorry for me behind my back."

Myrtle said, "Well, *I* didn't know anything about it, and I usually hear nearly everything that goes on here. So I don't think I'd worry about that."

Ellie said in a tired voice, "It's not just the public embarrassment. Now I'm wondering if maybe Mason was somehow involved in Victoria's death. And I can't stand myself for thinking that way. But obviously, I don't know Mason as well as I thought." She gave a hiccupping sigh.

"Is there anything particular that makes you think that? Did you see anything unusual at Victoria's party?"

Miles returned with a large glass of water, looking reluctant to enter again. He handed it to Ellie, who took a big sip.

Ellie was quiet for a couple of moments. "No, I didn't see anything at the party. But Mason was acting just so . . . weird. He was so tense on the drive over to Victoria's house. I thought he must have something work-related on his mind. I asked him about the renovation work, and he said Wisteria Hall was practically finished. Then he was silent the whole rest of the way. I was starting to think he was mad at me for some reason."

Myrtle said, "It sure sounds like he had other things on his mind. I didn't spend much time around Mason at the party. Did his mood improve?"

"He was just extremely quiet. Really reserved. And he seemed like he was trying to figure out what to say or how to act. Mason's not usually like that. I asked him at one point if he was feeling well."

"What was his answer to that?" asked Myrtle.

"He told me he was fine. Then, after that, he did strike up a conversation with Benton, which made me relieved. I thought maybe he'd just had a headache or something. It just wasn't like him."

Myrtle asked, "What *should* he have been like at the party?"

Ellie gave a small shrug. "Eager to show off the renovations. Proud. Maybe trying to sell the others on getting their own places renovated. Not quiet."

"What do you think was on his mind? His affair with Victoria? How was he acting around her?" asked Myrtle.

Ellie thought about this for a minute. "Mason was barely looking at her. I wondered if maybe there'd been some kind of disagreement between the two of them on a renovation issue. But now I'm thinking maybe Victoria was making life difficult for him. She kept trying to drag him into a conversation with her at the party. Calling out to him."

Myrtle said, "That seems an odd thing to do in front of your lover's wife."

"Yes. Which makes me wonder if maybe Victoria *wanted* me to find out about the affair. Maybe she hoped I'd divorce Mason if I found out."

Myrtle said, "Do you think Mason would have wanted that?"

Ellie frowned. "I need to confront Mason and ask him. I haven't done that yet because I'm worried what his answer might be. But I'm wondering if maybe he *didn't* want Victoria. Maybe he just wanted our boring old married life. After all, we're comfortable. We like spending time together. It's not exciting, but it's predictable. And there's something nice about predictable." She took another sip of water, as if her throat had suddenly gotten parched. "It makes me wonder if Mason murdered her. If he thought Victoria was trying to push him into something he didn't want."

Myrtle nodded at this. They were all quiet for a few moments. Miles looked longingly at the door of the studio as if he couldn't wait to escape again.

Myrtle said, "But what do you think happened to Adelaide?"

Ellie's brow creased. "That's what I don't understand. I could *sort of* see Mason murdering Victoria out of desperation. But Adelaide? Would Mason really kill an old lady? I just don't see it."

"Perhaps Adelaide saw something," said Myrtle gently. "If she had, Mason might have felt he had no choice."

Ellie sighed. "I have a really hard time believing he'd do it, even to keep himself out of jail. But I don't know. Like I said, now I'm feeling like I don't even know the man I married."

"You need to talk to Mason," said Myrtle firmly. "Tell him what you suspect. Give him the opportunity to explain himself. It may not be as bad as you think."

Ellie said ruefully, "Well, he definitely had an affair. But maybe he hasn't murdered anyone. I suppose that's something. But I just can't seem to speak to him about it." She looked up at Myrtle. "Could you?"

Miles made a startled grunt of dismay somewhere behind them.

"Of course I can. Miles and I would be happy to talk with Mason. But wouldn't you rather have someone else to do it, my dear? You're putting lots of trust in us."

Miles looked utterly miserable at this turn of events.

Ellie shook her head. "No. I'd like to think no one else knows, Miss Myrtle. And maybe they don't; you've helped convince me that maybe word hasn't really gotten out. Besides, you have a very no-nonsense manner. If you approach Mason, you'll get more information out of him."

Myrtle said, "Then Miles and I will go right away. And I'll report back to you, naturally." She paused. "I'm taking it you'd like to stay with Mason?"

"Yes. I think we can move ahead. As long as he's not a murderer, of course." Ellie gave a rather strangled laugh. "And thank you, both of you."

Chapter Twenty-Two

Miles held out his hand for his car keys as he and Myrtle headed to his car moments later.

"I'm wide awake now," he said grimly.

"Now, none of that was *my* fault, Miles. Ellie asked us to undertake a mission. We don't really have a choice."

"We had a choice about whether to come out here to speak with Ellie to begin with," said Miles.

"Yes. But now we're practically providing a community service. We're going to possibly save a marriage *and* help the town get to the bottom of the identity of a vicious killer." Myrtle was feeling very pleased with herself.

"I could use a break."

Myrtle was afraid if she granted Miles a break that it would be that much harder to get him out of his house again. He'd be like a rabbit in its warren. "I think we have an obligation to get this interview with Mason over with. After all, poor Ellie is sick with worry. The least we can do is relieve her mind."

"And if Mason is a two-time killer? How are we planning on defending ourselves?"

"There's safety in numbers," pointed out Myrtle. "I hardly think Mason can take on the both of us."

"We're old people," muttered Miles. "It wouldn't take a lot."

"Then let's meet him in public."

Miles said, "He's at work. He's probably in one of those little office sheds at some site."

"Then we'll invite him for a quick coffee at that spot downtown." Myrtle was pulling her phone out of her large purse as she spoke.

Miles stared at her before quickly training his eyes back on the road in front of him. "You're kidding."

"Not at all. You make an excellent point. We'll meet with him in a public setting." She tapped out a text with determination. "I'm sure he'll get right back to me."

Miles looked as if he were almost afraid to ask. "What did you text him?"

"*We know what you did. Meet Miles and me at the coffeehouse, pronto.*"

Miles said, "I need an aspirin."

She smiled. "He's already responded. He'll be there in five minutes."

By the time Myrtle and Miles settled themselves at a booth in the coffee shop, Mason, looking extremely harried, rushed into the building. He bypassed the counter completely, instead heading toward them with a look of fury and anxiety on his features. Miles shifted uncomfortably in the booth.

"For heaven's sake, Miles. It's not as if he's going to beat us up. He'd be subject to public fury. Possibly a hanging."

"The public might understand his point of view in this situation," said Miles in a low voice.

Mason sat across from them, spreading out his hands on the table. "What's going on? Are you trying to blackmail me?" He gave a short, barking laugh. "Imagine if I tell Red Clover that his mother is a petty criminal?"

Myrtle gave him a steady stare. "We would never do such a thing. Really, Mason. Miles and I are on a mission your wife sent us on."

"Ellie?" Mason looked confused and a little lost at the mention of her. He was quiet for a few moments. "Okay. Tell me."

So Myrtle filled him in quickly on their visit to the studio, the conversation with Ellie, her concerns, her tears. Then, for a few alarmed seconds, Myrtle feared Mason might start weeping himself.

But he could regain control, with some difficulty. He rubbed his face in exhaustion. "So Ellie knows about the affair. How did she find out?"

"We didn't inquire," said Myrtle pertly. "But wives often do have a sixth sense about these things. You probably weren't nearly as clever as you thought about covering it up. Or maybe Victoria *did* say something to her. She wanted to, as I'm sure she told you."

Mason took a deep breath. "Yeah, she wanted to. Victoria had some kind of crazy vision of the two of us making a life together at Wisteria Hall."

Miles was starting to relax as Mason's voice took a less aggressive tone. But Miles still clenched his coffee cup, perhaps prepared to fling its contents at Mason's face if things got out of hand.

"You didn't share this vision, did you?" asked Myrtle.

Mason shook his head emphatically. "I did not. I love Ellie. I must have been out of my mind to cheat on her." He gave Myrtle and Miles a searching look. "Does she want to leave me? What did she say?"

Myrtle said, "She'd like to stay with you, Mason. However, that's conditional."

"In what way?" he asked eagerly. "I'll do anything."

"Ellie, very wisely, wants to make sure you're not involved with Victoria's or Adelaide's murder."

Mason looked genuinely shocked. Then terrified. "You can't think I'd have anything to do with either of those. And Ellie . . . she couldn't believe that. There's no way."

But it sounded very much as if he were asking a question, not stating a fact.

"She just wants to make *sure*," repeated Myrtle.

Miles miserably swirled his coffee around in his cup.

Mason was quiet for a couple of moments. "Look, I'll admit to the affair. I don't know what I was thinking. It was a huge mistake. It's just that Victoria and I were spending a lot of time together at Wisteria Hall, managing the renovation project. It happened, and I'm not proud of it. I can tell you this, that affair was over and done with by the day of the party."

"Did Victoria realize that?" asked Myrtle.

Mason made an exasperated sound. "I don't know what Victoria realized. She was vain enough to believe I'd come back to her, I guess."

"Then, of course, there was the invitation to her party," said Myrtle.

"Yeah." Mason rubbed his face again. "Ellie got the mail that day. I'd have burned that invitation, believe me. But Ellie was pleased. If I'd have said I didn't want to go, Ellie would have been suspicious."

"Right," said Myrtle. "She'd have wondered why you'd turn down a friendly invitation from your biggest client. So you went."

"I did. But you have to realize that, at that point, I'd already called Victoria and broken everything off with her. It was over, like I said."

Myrtle said, "On the phone? Surely that wasn't very gentlemanly."

"It wasn't. I'm not proud of that. But you don't know how Victoria was. If I'd told her in person, she'd have gone off on me. It was bad enough on the phone."

Myrtle said, "And yet you still headed up the renovation."

"Yes," said Mason. "We had a contract for the work. Which unfortunately meant I was still going over to Wisteria Hall quite a bit. Victoria would tell me she wasn't going to allow me to end our affair."

Myrtle raised an eyebrow. "But it wasn't up to her, surely. Having an affair is a joint endeavor."

"Try telling Victoria that. She was a woman used to getting her own way."

Myrtle said, "So you were in a pretty bad situation, weren't you? You apparently wanted to remain married to Ellie."

"I didn't want to destroy my marriage."

Myrtle continued, "And yet the person you'd had the affair with was an important client."

Mason nodded.

"In some ways, your life became a bit easier when poor Victoria perished."

"No," said Mason quickly. "I mean, yes, obviously. I was sorry she was dead, but I admit I was glad in some ways that Ellie wouldn't find out about the affair. Victoria could be malevolent. I knew she might find a way to fill in Ellie. But I never touched that teacup."

Myrtle said, "Then there's Adelaide, of course."

"You're not trying to say I had anything to do with that."

Myrtle said, "Well, it's just that Adelaide lived directly next door to Wisteria Hall. She might have seen you over there. Maybe she said something to you about it."

Mason's eyebrows drew down. "I'm sure she *did* see me over there. I was over at Wisteria Hall all the time and for completely valid reasons."

"Maybe she spotted you over there one evening. Or maybe she saw the two of you embracing before you drove away one afternoon. There's no telling what she might have seen."

Mason threw up his hands. "As far as I'm aware, she didn't see anything. And didn't know anything. I certainly had nothing to do with her death. The woman taught me Latin, for heaven's sake. I'm not the kind of person who goes around murdering people."

"Where were you? Following the memorial service? Did you go by Wisteria Hall?"

Mason frowned. "Yes. But that was because of the job. There were still some things to wrap up. I told you that last time."

"Naturally, it's very close to Adelaide's house. It would have been easy to go over there and murder Adelaide."

Mason shook his head. "Not for me. It would never be easy for me to take the life of another person." He stood up. "I've got to get going." He hesitated. "If you see Ellie, tell her I love her." Then he hurried out the door.

Miles gave a sigh, looking exhausted.

"You were very quiet," noted Myrtle. Of course, she didn't think that was necessarily a bad thing. Sidekicks need to know their place.

"I was exceedingly uncomfortable," said Miles. He pushed his empty coffee cup away from him. "All this romantic intrigue. And it's really none of our business."

"Of course it's our business. We have a civic duty to return Bradley to the safe and happy town it usually is. Plus, I write for the newspaper. I plan on penning a big article on the resolution to these murders."

Miles sighed again. "What did you make of our chat with Mason?"

"It sounds to me like Victoria is completely the wrong person to have an affair with. In fact, it seems Victoria didn't totally understand the concept of an affair. She appeared to believe she and Mason had a future together."

Miles said, "Obviously, Mason didn't feel the same way."

"No. He thought he was engaging in a fling, didn't he? But Victoria didn't know how flings worked. Mason seems to love Ellie. He certainly wants to stay with her."

Myrtle tapped her coffee cup on the table, staring off into space.

"Should we get going?" asked Miles. "We're done for the day, aren't we? It feels like we've spoken with everybody." He shot a yearning look at the coffeehouse door.

Myrtle said, "I suppose. But something feels really off to me. Like I've forgotten to do something."

"I can't think what that is. You've been going through our usual routine of suspect interviews."

Myrtle brightened. "I know exactly what it is. I usually make someone a sympathy casserole."

Miles's face fell.

"The problem is that Victoria was single, and her brother left town before I could give him anything. Adelaide was single, too. Whatever family she has left is not in Bradley."

"Except for Puddin," said Miles wryly.

Myrtle said, "I don't think Puddin was exceptionally close to the Monroes. It seemed as if she washed her hands of the entire branch of the family. Really, she just took her family's lead on that. And no, I'm not making a casserole for Puddin." She looked over at Miles, frowning. "You seem rather pleased at the lack of casseroles."

"No, no. Not pleased. Just thinking about going home. It made me smile."

Myrtle gave him a suspicious look. Then she said slowly, "I could make Ellie a casserole. After all, she had quite a breakdown with us today, the poor thing."

"I don't think people give casseroles because of problematic marriages."

"Of course they do, Miles. People give casseroles for all sorts of reasons. In the South, if someone's having a hard time, they get a casserole. That's what I'll do, then. Give one to Ellie."

Miles said, "I'm done for today, Myrtle. I don't want to go over to Ellie's studio again. Not with a casserole or for any other reason."

"Then we'll go tomorrow."

Miles said, "Maybe Elaine would be a better choice to drive you. I have other things to do tomorrow."

"Other things? What other things?"

"Chess," said Miles quickly. "I have chess club tomorrow."

"Do you? How extraordinarily inconvenient."

Miles said, "Maybe you can ask Elaine to take you. It'll give you more time with Jack."

"I suppose I could. But how very annoying."

Minutes later, Miles was dropping Myrtle off at her house. He gave her what looked like a relieved wave as he headed home.

Myrtle let herself into her house and into the kitchen. There she proceeded to review everything she'd recently purchased at the Piggly Wiggly. Remarkably, there didn't seem much to make a meal from.

Looking for inspiration, she found her mother's old recipe box. The cards were faded, stained, and creased, but Myrtle still preferred them to the cookbooks she had. She narrowed her eyes as she flipped through the cards. She finally settled on funeral potato casserole.

Reading through the ingredients, Myrtle realized she would need to improvise. She heard a scratching at her kitchen window and absently opened it to allow Pasha to leap in. "Darling Pasha. Here to give me a hand?"

Pasha perched on a kitchen stool, swishing her tail in agreement.

"I believe some improvisation with this recipe is going to be necessary," said Myrtle.

Pasha narrowed her green eyes.

"Cottage Cheese will work instead of sour cream."

Pasha seemed willing to allow the substitution.

"There's no heavy cream here. But I do have evaporated milk. Milk is milk, after all. Evaporated just means it's concentrated, which sounds better anyway."

Pasha looked less certain about this.

Myrtle tsked. "I forgot butter at the store. But I do have bacon grease I saved in a jar."

Pasha turned away.

Myrtle went to work. She couldn't find an appropriately sized casserole dish, so she used a smaller one. Since everyone likes bacon, she added the bacon grease generously. Because she was out of breadcrumbs, she added crushed corn flakes. "It's all carbohydrates," she muttered.

Pasha's gaze followed again as Myrtle pulled out cayenne pepper instead of paprika. Pasha blinked.

"Maybe Elaine can take me over to Ellie's this afternoon," Myrtle said to Pasha. "In which case I should whip this up faster than not. Let's do 450 degrees instead of 350."

The casserole thus concocted, Myrtle and Pasha settled in the living room. Myrtle worked on a crossword while Pasha napped in her lap.

It wasn't terribly long before the smoke detector went off. Pasha fled in alarm as Myrtle rushed into her kitchen. There was black smoke everywhere. Myrtle pulled open the oven door to find the top of the casserole blackened, its edges bubbling over in a greasy mess burning off the bottom of the appliance.

"Mercy," she muttered. "What on earth happened?"

She gingerly pulled the dish from the oven, setting it on a hot plate. Then she waved a cookie sheet, which should perhaps have been under the casserole dish to begin with, in the air until the smoke detector stopped. She could hear crowing in the distance as Scotty registered his displeasure at the noise.

Pasha peeked around the corner of the kitchen door.

"All is well," said Myrtle in a reassuring voice. "And I'm fairly sure I can scrape off the top layer. It'll be fine underneath."

Pasha's eyes narrowed.

"You think I should try a bite of it?" asked Myrtle with a frown.

Pasha fixed her with an unblinking stare.

"I suppose I could. It isn't something I ordinarily do. I want to leave as much as possible for the casserole recipient."

But Pasha's gaze was unrelenting. Myrtle took out a spoon, dipping it into the bottom of the dish and avoiding the scorched top. She blew on the contents of the spoon to cool it for quite some time before taking a bite. She started coughing.

Pasha watched her, eyes inscrutable.

Myrtle drank water straight from the tap, still coughing in between sips. "Mercy," she said again when she could talk.

"My mother apparently couldn't cook," said Myrtle, frowning at the recipe card. "This is inedible."

Pasha seemed to agree.

"I'll deal with it later. Maybe I can add more bacon grease to make it palatable." She wrapped it loosely in aluminum foil and shoved it into the refrigerator. Then she made an attempt to clean the kitchen.

"Perhaps I should open the windows and let the house air out a bit."

Pasha seemed to agree with this. Myrtle settled back again in her chair with her crossword. Pasha decided to have a bath across the room. She appeared to be blocking the door to the kitchen in case Myrtle felt she needed to try to remedy the casserole again.

But Myrtle couldn't focus on the crossword. The suspects and their various motives kept wending their way through her mind. She took out a small notebook from the table next to her chair and jotted a few notes. She mentioned Walter, with his inn and family legacy. Then she wrote about Benton and Tippy and Victoria's pressure regarding zoning and permits. Mason was next with his affair and the way Victoria was practically blackmailing him to continue it. Then there was Ellie with her knowledge about the affair.

The phone rang, and Myrtle grabbed it. It was Wanda.

"They think I dunnit."

Myrtle frowned. "That you've done what?"

"Killed Victoria. Yer boy just left here after grillin' me for near about an hour."

"Red questioned you? That's absurd."

"Wanted to know why I went up to the widda's walk."

Myrtle snorted. "I already told him why."

"Didn't seem to make no difference." Wanda's voice was flat, matter-of-fact. "Reckon findin' the body makes me look guilty."

"They're fishing in the wrong pond."

"Mebbe so. But they're fishin' real hard in this one."

"Don't worry. You didn't do anything, so you won't be a suspect for long. I'm glad you called; you've been on my mind. I suppose you know what happened to Adelaide."

Wanda said sadly on the other end, "Yep. Reckon she knew too much."

"How are things with you? You seemed very depleted after the night at Wisteria Hall. Have you managed to recuperate?"

"I done all right. But this bad feelin' won't go away. Yer in danger."

"Yes. But don't worry. Miles and I are just gathering information. It's been a rather eventful day. I'm sure we're narrowing in on the killer. It's just a matter of time."

Wanda still sounded uneasy despite Myrtle's assurances. "Don't feel right about it."

"I'll be careful."

"Real careful, Myrtle."

After hanging up, Myrtle felt unsettled. But then, that was likely the entire reason for Wanda's call. Wanda seemed to think Myrtle wasn't cautious enough. Well, she was certainly feeling cautious now. Pasha asked to go out, which Myrtle granted. Then she closed her windows and checked to make sure the doors were locked.

It was quite a while later when Myrtle finally turned in. She tossed and turned, thinking over the events of the day. Finally,

she fell into a restless sleep, dreaming of hidden passages and secret rooms.

Chapter Twenty-Three

The next morning, Myrtle was up at three. She read until dawn while fortifying herself with a pot of strong coffee.

"So, Benton this morning," she muttered to herself. She dressed, choosing sensible shoes and her largest purse so she could carry her notebook with her. She gave herself a critical look in the full-length mirror. "Perfect. Just an old lady asking questions." It was a role she was well-acquainted with.

It was 7:45 when she called Miles. He answered, sounding groggy. "Is it morning?"

"Apparently not for you," said Myrtle rather caustically. "I thought we were going to go see Benton."

"Maybe at ten? I might make it at ten."

Myrtle said, "I'm starting to think you have mono or something. You've been very sleepy during this case."

"Trying to wean myself off caffeine."

"For heaven's sake. No wonder. What were you drinking in the coffeehouse yesterday?"

Miles said with a yawn, "Decaf."

"Ugh. Well, I would imagine it would take a person quite a few days to adjust to life without caffeine. Perhaps it would be better if you got more shuteye, Miles."

"Really?" Miles sounded as if he'd been given a very unexpected gift.

"Yes. Seeing Benton is hardly a big deal."

"Elaine should be able to drive you, right?"

Myrtle said, "No need. As you know, town hall isn't a long walk. It's a pretty day. I'll take in the fall weather."

There was a brisk breeze blowing as she walked toward downtown. There were a few leaves that had turned color and fell earlier than the rest, and Myrtle plowed through them as she went.

A police car pulled alongside her. It was Red. He rolled down his window.

"Where you heading, Mama?" he frowned at her.

"Just for a little stroll. Nothing exciting. It's a lovely day."

"It's kind of a windy, chilly day. Not a great day for a walk." Now Red looked even more suspicious. "You wouldn't be working on the case, would you?"

"Certainly not! How suspicious you are, Red. It's important to get lots of daily steps, they say. For your health."

"How about if I drive you wherever you're heading?" he asked.

"That would prevent me from getting exercise. Really, it's a very simple concept." She had no desire to ask her son to drop her off at town hall.

Luckily, Red's phone rang. He glanced at the screen and said, "Okay, Mama. But be careful." He drove off.

What with Wanda's remonstrations on top of Red's it's a wonder Myrtle felt confident walking anywhere alone. But she made her way to town hall fairly quickly. She walked up to the receptionist in the planning office. "Good morning. I need to speak with Benton, please."

"Do you have an appointment?" asked the young woman sweetly.

"No, but I'm with the *Bradley Bugle*. I'm confirming some information for an article." She paused. "And you know how much Benton likes publicity."

"Mr. Chambers is very busy this morning. Perhaps you could call later or send an email?"

Myrtle scowled. Then she spotted that Benton's door was open. She could hear voices coming from within. "Is he in a meeting?"

"Yes, with Mr. Beaumont from The Bradley Inn."

Myrtle said brightly, "Perfect! I should probably speak with Walter, too. I'll just pop in."

"Mrs. Clover! You'll really need to come back later."

Myrtle gave her a severe look. Perhaps another tack was in order. "It's not just about the article. Tippy also asked me to co-ordinate Adelaide Monroe's memorial service with Benton."

The young woman frowned. "It's my understanding Mrs. Chambers is handling that herself."

Myrtle thought this receptionist was being entirely too ob-structive. She also seemed to know far too much about Tippy's activities. "She was. But she ended up having to delegate. You know how busy Tippy is."

No one could argue with that. Tippy was the busiest person Myrtle knew.

"Oh. Well, I suppose that's important. But please keep it brief. Mr. Chambers has a planning commission meeting at nine."

"I'll be quick as a flash," said Myrtle, heading to Benton's office.

Once in the inner sanctum, she beamed at Benton and Walter. "Good morning! How fortuitous to find you both here."

Benton's face fell. Walter looked startled, almost guilty. Walter half-rose from his chair before plopping back down again. Myrtle sat in a leather chair next to Walter's and across a large desk where Benton frowned at her from the other side.

"Myrtle. What are you doing here?"

Myrtle smiled at him. "I wanted to speak with you about poor Adelaide's death. Tippy wants to do a memorial service for her, seeing as how she doesn't have any local family. Or perhaps, no family left at all. It's hard to remember which."

Benton pressed his lips together in irritation. "Shouldn't that be something you navigate with Tippy? I don't have anything to do with that."

"No, I suppose you wouldn't. But I wanted to check in with you also and see how Tippy was holding up. She seemed very upset at Adelaide's death. Most upset, actually."

Benton gave a gusty sigh. "Well, Tippy's a very sensitive person. She's holding up all right." He looked at his watch in a performative way.

"I suppose you must have known Adelaide quite well, yourself. Her family has been so important locally for so long. Rather like Walter's family." Myrtle gave Walter a big grin. He gave her a nervous smile in return.

Myrtle said, "Tippy mentioned a memory table with photos for Adelaide's service. We could ask people to bring old photos of the Monroes. Anything with Adelaide in it, of course."

Benton made a tight smile. "Nice idea."

"And I'll keep it in mind, too," said Walter, standing in a rush. "I really should be getting along. Benton, it was good to see you." He hurriedly walked out.

Benton seemed to look for ways to make this unexpected meeting with Myrtle wrap up as quickly as possible. "Yes, terrible news about Adelaide."

Myrtle said, "Where were you when you heard the news? After Victoria's memorial service, where did you go?"

Benton's face flushed with annoyance, whether at being questioned or because Myrtle simply got under his skin, it was difficult to discern. "I went back to town hall. I needed to get some work done. I've been absolutely swamped at my job lately." He gave another pointed glance at his watch.

"I see. So you didn't go see Adelaide."

"Of course not. What makes you think I would?"

Myrtle shrugged, "Oh, I don't know. It seems as if she was spending time thinking about how to block Victoria's permits, after all. Maybe you were visiting her regarding permits."

"Now, Miss Myrtle. I went nowhere near Adelaide Monroe's house. Like I said, I came here to town hall to work. Which is what I should be doing right now," he added meaningfully.

But Myrtle ignored the hint. "I've also been thinking about that dreadful party."

Benton made a face. "I wish we'd never gone to it."

"What *did* make you and Tippy decide to go? It seems like you'd have realized that she'd use the occasion to put pressure on you both to green-light the permits and zoning."

Benton said, "Tippy thought we should go." He frowned. "I'm not exactly sure what you were doing there. Or Miles."

"We're friends of Wanda."

"Who?" asked Benton, frowning.

"The psychic."

"Oh, right, right," said Benton. He rolled his eyes. "Victoria wanted to market Wisteria Hall as haunted, I think. I guess she was taking the idea out for a test run. Balderdash."

Myrtle changed tack. "I've been wondering what you made of all this. After all, you know all the guests at the party. I'm sure the police informed you this was murder. Do you have any insights as to who might have wanted Victoria out of the way?"

Benton was quiet for a few moments, taking the question seriously. "I've been thinking about that. Mason might have wanted Victoria gone."

Myrtle affected surprise at this. "Mason? But she'd given him that lucrative contract to renovate her home."

"Yeah, but that wasn't the full story." He paused, apparently trying to come up with an appropriate wording for Myrtle's delicate, senior ears. "Mason and Victoria were an item. I found out about it when I overheard her talking to him on the phone one day. Maybe the affair didn't work out, and Victoria was creating problems for him."

Myrtle nodded. "That does make sense, doesn't it? Of course, Walter Beaumont also has quite a bit of motive."

Benton looked more uncomfortable at this scenario. Perhaps it was because Walter had just left his office minutes before. "I suppose so. But I feel for the man. He's working so hard to continue with the inn. He's at town hall all the time to ask about grants for historic buildings and whatnot. He's taken out a loan. Walter is doing everything he can to preserve his family's legacy." He tapped his thick fingers on the desk. "I just can't picture it."

Then Benton frowned. "Maybe you can answer a question for me. How does Red think Victoria was murdered? Tippy says there was no sign of violence against Victoria that she noticed. Do they think someone followed Victoria up to the roof after the lights went out? Because we were all right there. Was it poison?"

Myrtle shook her head. "You know Red never confides in me, Benton. I'm the last person he'd say anything to."

"If somebody *did* follow Victoria up to the roof, it must have been one of the staff," said Benton in a decisive voice. "That means the police are just asking all of the guests questions because of protocol, not because we're actually suspects." He sounded quite relieved at this prospect.

Myrtle burst his bubble. "I don't think the police believe it's the staff. Besides, who would kill Adelaide, if that was the case?"

"Two different murderers?" asked Benton hopefully.

"That's unlikely, surely. Especially considering both victims were at the same party."

Benton said, "Then Adelaide saw something. The staff member decided to silence her."

"Fiddlesticks. That makes no sense at all. Adelaide was in the conservatory or the living room the entire time. If a member of the catering staff killed Victoria, Adelaide would know nothing about it. No. The only explanation is that Victoria was poisoned. And Adelaide knew something."

And, just then, Myrtle realized something. When she'd been speaking with Mason, he'd said something about a teacup. How on earth did Mason know the teacup was the delivery method for the poison?

Now Myrtle was ready for her tête-à-tête with Benton to be over. She picked up her purse and her cane and said, "I should really be going. Tell Tippy I said hi."

Her mind was completely consumed by Mason now as she hurried back toward home, her cane thumping on the sidewalk. Mason and the teacup. Mason and the affair. And Mason, who allegedly had nightshade in his own garden at home.

She pulled her phone out of her large purse to call Miles, unable to keep this key bit of information to herself. Sadly, this resulted in her dropping the purse altogether, its contents scattering all over the sidewalk. "For heaven's sake," she muttered. As she stooped to retrieve everything, she dropped her cane. "Fiddlesticks."

A car pulled alongside her, parking at the curb. "Miss Myrtle?" called Walter. "Are you all right?"

Chapter Twenty-Four

"Yes, yes, I'm fine. But the contents of my purse are spread everywhere. Ridiculous. I get over-excited sometimes and drop things. Thanks for helping, Walter. Everything in that purse is absolutely essential."

Walter, politely, didn't dispute this as he carefully picked up band-aids, grocery lists, a capless lipstick, loose change, rubber bands, hard candies, obituaries snipped from the newspaper, a partially completed crossword puzzle, and an expired coupon from the Piggly Wiggly. He put them all safely back in her enormous handbag.

"That's a well-constructed purse," he said courteously.

"Isn't it? I got it in the 1980s. It's still completely serviceable."

Walter said, "Let me give you a lift home, Miss Myrtle. I was going to bring you some pictures, anyway."

"Hmm?"

"Pictures," said Walter a little louder, in case Myrtle was harder of hearing than he'd suspected. "For Adelaide's memory table."

Myrtle had forgotten again about the table. She was wishing she had said nothing at all about it. "All right then," she said rather ungraciously. "That sounds good."

"Do you need a hand?" asked Walter, frowning at the problem of how to get Myrtle into his pickup truck.

"No. That's a benefit of being quite tall." As a matter of fact, she was taller than Walter. She climbed into the truck, a 1990s-model pickup, and they set off on the short drive to Myrtle's house.

Walter pointed to a large envelope on the floor next to her feet. "The photos are in there. Actually, it's a relief that I'm unloading some of these things. As you might imagine, there are lots of Beaumont pictures. I've given them away as often as possible since my kids don't seem that interested in family history. The historical society has taken some of them off my hands."

Myrtle opened the envelope to find pictures of the Monroes with the Beaumonts at various functions through the decades. Potlucks, cookouts, and days at the lake. Her heart sank as she realized she was now the keeper of these things. Walter certainly didn't want them back. Perhaps she could fob them off on Tippy.

She was so absorbed in thinking about the Monroe pictures that she didn't notice Walter had continued talking. "What?" she asked.

Walter said patiently, again in that louder tone because of Myrtle's assumed deafness, "I can identify everyone in the photos for you. It might be fun to have a series on Bradley's history in pictures for the newspaper."

Myrtle brightened. Of course, the *Bradley Bugle*'s archives. That would be the perfect final resting place for the assorted Monroe photos that were surely coming in her direction. Sadly, she couldn't escape a visit with Walter, who'd undoubtedly walk her through every picture in his collection. There was nothing that could be done about it.

So they walked inside Myrtle's house minutes later, Myrtle still thinking about how Mason had mentioned the teacup. The teacup he shouldn't have known about.

Walter happily spread out the pictures on her coffee table, already pointing out some especially tiresome photos of Adelaide with his mother at some sort of Christmas party. "Our families were always close. It seems like the old days used to be so much simpler than now."

Myrtle supposed it was easy to feel that way if you'd only recently fallen on hard times. She'd never had any money to lose, so didn't relate.

Walter was now looking sadly at a photo of Adelaide during a Halloween costume party. "We all did have a lot of fun. I hate that she's gone now."

"It's the end of an era, isn't it?"

Walter said, "She seemed sort of troubled lately. Adelaide, I mean."

"Did she? Well, it was probably about Victoria's murder, wasn't it? We've all been troubled by that."

Walter nodded. "You and Adelaide spoke for a while at Victoria's memorial service. Did she share what was on her mind at all?"

"Hmm? No, not really. We discussed old times and so forth."

Walter pushed, "Nothing else? Nothing about the party?"

Myrtle frowned. "Do you think she knew something about the party, then?"

"I was wondering if that's why she was murdered. If she'd seen something."

Myrtle's eyes narrowed. What was Walter getting at? Was he simply being nosy? Or was he pressing to see what Myrtle knew? She decided to test him, but from a bit of a distance.

"I'm going to get us some food."

Walter said, "Oh, I'm fine, Miss Myrtle."

"Then I'll get myself some. I could use a nibble."

Once safely in the kitchen and getting a plate, she called back, "As a matter of fact, Adelaide did mention seeing something happen at the table while everyone was at the buffet."

Walter was quiet for a moment. "Did she?"

"That's right. Something to do with a teacup. But our conversation was interrupted."

Walter was suddenly in the kitchen with her as Myrtle opened the fridge door. "She didn't say what she saw?"

Myrtle reached into the refrigerator. "I believe she might have seen you, Walter. Did she?"

Walter made a cornered, snarling sound like a trapped animal.

Myrtle carefully took out her funeral potatoes, trying to act more casual than she felt. "What did she see, exactly? Did you have a vial? A vial with some nightshade poison inside? Everyone was so busy with the buffet and the teacups were all nicely labeled so they could be party favors. You must have thought that was a real stroke of luck, didn't you? You knew exactly which cup was Victoria's."

The funeral potatoes were quite heavy. Myrtle rested them lightly on the counter, her hands still gripping the handles of the glass container.

Walter said, "Adelaide thought I was drinking. That I had some sort of problem. I could tell she was embarrassed."

"*I* see. Adelaide saw you with the vial, but thought it was some sort of flask. That you'd been driven to drink because of all the financial problems you'd experienced with The Bradley Inn."

Walter spread out his hands in an imploring gesture. "The inn is all I have. And Victoria was stealing my staff, undercutting my business. That was just the beginning of it. When she finally opened up the bed-and-breakfast, complete with ghost tours and whatever else, I was going to be ruined."

"I understand she made an offer on the inn."

Walter gave a short laugh. "That was totally insulting. She wanted to buy me out but give me pennies on the dollar for what it's worth."

Myrtle gave an understanding nod. "It must have been a nightmare. But it's all over now, Walter. Let's give Red a little call."

Walter gave her an uncomprehending look. "No. No way. I've worked too hard. You're thinking I'll just give up and go to *prison*? Absolutely not."

"Think about it. I'm sure one passer-by will have seen you helping me with my spilled purse. If I come to a violent end, people will piece it together. *Red* will piece it together." She tried to edge past him, but Walter blocked her way. She was now cornered against the kitchen wall.

"Don't be foolish, Walter. You're only making things worse."

He shook his head. "They'll think it's a break-in. A robbery."

Myrtle laughed. "Really? Surely you don't think any self-respecting burglar would imagine I have anything valuable in this house."

Walter lunged at her.

Myrtle swung the funeral potatoes at him.

Chapter Twenty-Five

Walter gave a howl as he stumbled backward, covered with paprika-smothered potatoes, and crashed into the kitchen table. The casserole dish smashed on the floor, glass scattering everywhere.

Myrtle fled for the front door, cane thumping frantically as she went. She fumbled with the door handle, finally opening it and hurrying into the yard. "Help!" she yelled. "Murderer! Help!"

She spotted Miles coming out of his house. "Get a weapon, Miles!" Then she spotted Erma on her front porch, ever the nosy neighbor. "Call Red, Erma!"

Then Scotty the rooster exploded onto the scene in a flurry of feathers and fury. Walter had made it out into the yard, blind with fury, Myrtle in his sights.

Scotty took exception to Walter in every way. Perhaps it was the paprika-peppered funeral potatoes that made him so agitated. At any rate, he flew at Walter, flapping at his face, pecking at his legs. Walter tried fending off the rooster, yelling at it. The yelling only increased the wretched beast's disquiet, and it escalated its attack.

"Get it off me!" screamed Walter.

Myrtle couldn't seem to summon any sympathy for him.

By this point, Erma and Miles had reached Myrtle's yard. Elaine was just behind, looking very embarrassed. "I'm *so* sorry," she said before crooning at Scotty as if he were a tantrum-throwing toddler.

Red was right behind her, a sandwich in his hand, the remains of which he stuffed into his mouth as he jogged over to help. While he chewed, he was glaring at Myrtle as if it were all her fault. Which it most certainly wasn't.

Red grabbed the rooster, but not Walter, which was not the correct choice. Walter, to be fair, wasn't looking very good. He was bleeding from the hit by the funeral potatoes, covered with food, and was scratched and pecked by the wrathful rooster.

Elaine was still profusely apologizing for Scotty's egregious behavior. Red handed her the chicken, then frowned at Walter. "Okay," he drawled. "You're covered with food." He leaned forward, delicately sniffing the air. "You're covered with really bad food." He turned to look at Myrtle. She gave him a scowl in return.

Miles was hovering in the background, looking at Myrtle with concern. He cleared his throat. "I believe that's Myrtle's casserole."

"Yes," agreed Red. "I believe it must be." His eyes narrowed at Walter. "I'd like to know exactly why my mother covered you with her infamous funeral potatoes."

Myrtle smiled smugly to herself. She wasn't about to interject. Walter, being Walter, would likely implicate himself while he was trying to stammer out an excuse. And suddenly, Wanda's vision of broken glass and old photographs made perfect sense.

Walter indeed appeared flustered. He looked anxiously at Myrtle, who shrugged and stayed silent in response. Finally, he decided on what he thought was a reasonable explanation. "I brought over photos for Adelaide's memorial service. Your mother is collecting them. The Monroes and Beaumonts have been friends for decades."

"Hmm," said Red. "Interesting. Still doesn't explain the food."

"She threw it at me," admitted Walter.

"Did she now? That seems like unusual behavior for my mother."

Walter began perspiring profusely. "She . . . I think she has dementia, Red. I'm sorry to say it. You're always talking about putting her in Greener Pastures Retirement Home, and you're right. She needs to go."

Red raised his eyebrows. "Is that so?" He looked over at Myrtle, who was now focused on Walter with a good degree of animosity.

Walter bobbed his head in several quick nods. "It is."

"You see," said Red slowly, "there are many reasons I want Mama in a home. But dementia isn't one of them. She's clear as a bell. As a matter of fact, she's playing with more marbles than anyone else I know. So that right there tells me you're lying, Walter. I'm going to ask you again. Why did my mother throw her casserole at you? And how did you both end up outdoors afterward? Because it sure seems like she was trying to defend herself and then fleeing from you."

Walter opened and closed his mouth a few times, looking like a fish that's been brought up on a line. Then he sagged, enough that Red put out a hand to steady him.

"I did it," he finally said.

Miles breathed out a loud sigh.

"What exactly did you do?" pressed Red.

"I . . . well, I'm responsible for Victoria and Adelaide's deaths."

Now, Myrtle was happy to join in. "You *killed* them, Walter. You're not just *responsible* for them. You cold-bloodedly murdered them to protect your inn from going under."

Walter nodded miserably again. "Yes."

"Tell me a little about that," said Red before quickly reading Walter his rights.

Walter didn't seem to listen. In fact, it was almost as if he were in his own little world. Perhaps the incident with the rooster had unbalanced him, or maybe he'd already been unbalanced prior to that. He said, "The inn wasn't going to survive. Victoria was making sure of that. She'd taken my staff. She was going to open a much more luxurious bed-and-breakfast."

Myrtle added, "Plus, there was the insulting offer to buy The Bradley Inn."

"Yes." Walter's face flushed, thinking about it. "The inn was going to be sunk. And my dad tasked me with keeping the inn open when he was on his death bed. He asked me to swear to keep it going for the next generation."

Red said dryly, "I don't think he intended you to stoop to murder."

Walter didn't seem to hear him. He continued, "When I got that party invitation, it was like Victoria was rubbing her bed-and-breakfast in my face. I couldn't help myself."

Myrtle said sternly, "You could certainly help yourself, Walter. It wasn't as if this crime was committed in the heat of the moment. You planned it out. You brought nightshade poison in a vial to tamper with Victoria's drink. This was a well-thought-out murder."

Red was still watching Walter with narrowed eyes.

Walter said, "I didn't want her to suffer. I'm not that kind of person. I just wanted her out of the way. Poison seemed like the best way to do it."

"Surely you don't have nightshade at the inn," said Myrtle.

"No. That wouldn't be good for liability reasons. I've seen nightshade in a neighbor's yard. It was easy enough to grab it. I figured a party would be a good place to put the poison in her glass. She'd be distracted, and there would be lots of suspects.

Myrtle interjected again. "But it was risky having people around. And Adelaide saw you."

Walter cleared his throat. "Adelaide saw me with a *vial*. She didn't see me putting anything in Victoria's cup."

Red said, "Must have been a real stroke of luck that everybody had personalized teacups."

"Yes," said Walter. "I didn't have to worry about accidentally poisoning someone else." He looked back at Myrtle again. "Anyway, Adelaide thought I was drinking. That it was a flask of whiskey or something. She felt sorry for me."

"But later," said Myrtle, "she got to thinking. If Victoria had been poisoned, it might have been a vial of poison she saw, not a flask. I'm guessing she wanted to ask you in person, though. She was trying to give you the benefit of the doubt, wasn't she? After all, as you just mentioned, the Monroes and the Beaumonts have been friends for decades. She didn't think you were a killer. But after the memorial service, you proved you were. You killed Adelaide with a decorative stone."

Walter quickly said, "She didn't suffer. She never even knew what hit her."

"As if that makes things better," said Myrtle with a sniff. "Poor Adelaide is dead before her time."

Red pulled out his handcuffs. "Okay, let's move this to the station. I've got to let Perkins and the rest of the team know. I'll need you to sign a formal confession."

Walter nodded miserably. "Are the handcuffs really necessary?"

"Oh, I think they are," said Red in a grim voice. "Don't think I don't remember you just tried to kill my mother."

As they walked across the street to Red's police car, Red called out, "Miles? Will you see about Mama?"

"Will do," said Miles. For a moment, it seemed as if he might salute in response. Then, to Myrtle, he said, "Let's head inside. More sherry might be in order."

Several neighbors had emerged from their houses, drawn by the commotion. Erma held court in the middle of the street, gesturing dramatically. "And then the rooster attacked! I've never seen anything like it. My digestive system was in absolute turmoil. I thought my irritable bowel was going to act up right then and there."

Elaine was still holding Scotty, who was now preening, looking quite pleased with himself. "Myrtle, I'll come over with Jack and help you clean up inside. Sounds like there are potatoes on the floor?"

"Don't bother," said Myrtle. "Look who's here."

And indeed, Puddin just pulled into Myrtle's driveway, an avid expression on her pale features.

Puddin ended up cleaning up the funeral potatoes, lured by the story of how Myrtle had made a narrow escape and the story of the downfall of Walter Beaumont. After all, Puddin was a Monroe herself and relished the story of a family friend turned vicious killer.

Myrtle, after a small glass of sherry, wrote a story for the *Bradley Bugle* that resulted in many extra copies sold at the Piggly Wiggly and quite a few extra subscriptions to the paper.

Several days later, Myrtle looked out her window with satisfaction. Dusty was mowing her lawn, having first stowed her gnomes in the shed for the next time Red stepped out of line. Red's defense of her in front of Walter had resulted in the gnomes' temporary removal. For now, at least.

Myrtle turned to sit back again across from Miles, who was sipping a lemonade. Pasha, who'd been watching Myrtle intently, leaped into her lap. "So, everything's back to normal?" he asked.

"That's right," she said with satisfaction, rubbing Pasha on her head. The cat purred at her.

"You seemed to have had quite a few visitors in the last few days," he noted.

"Yes. Everyone was exceedingly nosy. Most of the other suspects came over to speak with me. This allowed me to be nosy in return, of course."

Miles nodded. "What did you find out?"

"Mason and Ellie are working on their marriage. Ellie, as she said, was willing to stick around as long as Mason was just a cheater, not a murderer."

Miles said, "And how did Mason know Victoria's teacup was poisoned? You mentioned earlier that was a red herring."

"Yes. He'd just surmised it was poison, considering no one had followed Victoria out of the room. Apparently, Mason is good at deductions. And Benton was relieved it was all over."

Miles raised his eyebrows. "Benton actually came by to check on you?"

"Goodness, no. He sent Tippy as his emissary. But she said he was glad to get back to life as usual. Oh, and her memorial service for Adelaide is this weekend. It sounds very well thought-out."

Miles said, "I'd expect nothing less."

"Wisteria Hall is up for sale. Victoria's brother has no interest in being in the hospitality business, especially remotely. I'll be curious to see what happens there."

"What about The Bradley Inn?" asked Miles. "What's going to happen to it? Walter had said his kids weren't interested in running it."

"They're apparently not, no. It's also for sale. I suppose a buyer could come through for both the inn and Wisteria Hall. Or perhaps the same buyer. After all, one's an inn, one's a bed-and-breakfast." Myrtle paused. "Oh, and Elaine found a home on a real farm for Scotty. He's apparently living his best life there, bossing all the hens and other roosters around."

"Well, the bird was a threat to the neighborhood. And quite the escape artist."

"Indeed he was," said Myrtle. "Bless his little heart."

Miles said, "Well, that's that, then. Peace is restored to Bradley."

"Until next time," murmured Myrtle with satisfaction.

About the Author

Bestselling cozy mystery author Elizabeth Spann Craig is a library-loving, avid mystery reader. A pet-owning Southerner, her four series are full of cats, corgis, and cheese grits. The mother of two, she lives with her husband, a fun-loving corgi, and a couple of cute cats.

Sign up for Elizabeth's free newsletter to stay updated on releases:

https://bit.ly/2xZUXqO

This and That

A special thanks to Rebecca Wahr for her invaluable rooster tales and information!

I love hearing from my readers. You can find me on Facebook as Elizabeth Spann Craig Author, on Twitter as elizabethscraig, on my website at elizabethspanncraig.com, and by email at elizabethspanncraig@gmail.com.

Thanks so much for reading my book...I appreciate it. If you enjoyed the story, would you please leave a short review on the site where you purchased it? Just a few words would be great. Not only do I feel encouraged reading them, but they also help other readers discover my books. Thank you!

Did you know my books are available in print and ebook formats? Most of the Myrtle Clover series is available in audio and some of the Southern Quilting mysteries are. Find the audiobooks here: https://elizabethspanncraig.com/audio/

Please follow me on BookBub for my reading recommendations and release notifications.

I'd also like to thank some folks who helped me put this book together. Thanks to my cover designer, Karri Klawiter, for her awesome covers. Thanks to my editor, Judy Beatty for her help. Thanks to beta readers Amanda Arrieta, Rebecca Wahr, Cassie Kelley, and Dan Harris for all of their helpful suggestions and careful reading. Thanks to my ARC readers for helping to spread the word. Thanks, as always, to my family and readers.

Other Works by Elizabeth

Myrtle Clover Series in Order (be sure to look for the Myrtle series in audio, ebook, and print):

Pretty is as Pretty Dies

Progressive Dinner Deadly

A Dyeing Shame

A Body in the Backyard

Death at a Drop-In

A Body at Book Club

Death Pays a Visit

A Body at Bunco

Murder on Opening Night

Cruising for Murder

Cooking is Murder

A Body in the Trunk

Cleaning is Murder

Edit to Death

Hushed Up

A Body in the Attic

Murder on the Ballot

Death of a Suitor

A Dash of Murder
Death at a Diner
A Myrtle Clover Christmas
Murder at a Yard Sale
Doom and Bloom
A Toast to Murder

Mystery Loves Company
A Murder Down Memory Lane
Murder Sees All

The Village Library Mysteries in Order:
Checked Out
Overdue
Borrowed Time
Hush-Hush
Where There's a Will
Frictional Characters
Spine Tingling
A Novel Idea
End of Story
Booked Up
Out of Circulation
Shelf Life
Dead Silence
The Sunset Ridge Mysteries in Order
The Type-A Guide to Solving Murder
The Type-A Guide to Dinner Parties
Southern Quilting Mysteries in Order:
Quilt or Innocence

Knot What it Seams
Quilt Trip
Shear Trouble
Tying the Knot
Patch of Trouble
Fall to Pieces
Rest in Pieces
On Pins and Needles
Fit to be Tied
Embroidering the Truth
Knot a Clue
Quilt-Ridden
Needled to Death
A Notion to Murder
Crosspatch
Behind the Seams
Quilt Complex
A Southern Quilting Cozy Christmas

Memphis Barbeque Mysteries in Order (Written as Riley Adams):
Delicious and Suspicious
Finger Lickin' Dead
Hickory Smoked Homicide
Rubbed Out

And a standalone "cozy zombie" novel: Race to Refuge, written as Liz Craig